DESPERATE DEEDS

Tales of Triumph and...

last date shown below

A D R I A N   J A C

General Editor: G

CollinsEducatio
An imprint of HarperCollins

but
pleas

ISBN 0 00 323031 7

First published by CollinsEducational, *an imprint of* HarperCollins *Publishers* 77-85 Fulham Palace Road, London W6 8JB.

Cover and text designed by Christie Archer
Cover illustration by Neil Dishington
Edited by Stephen Attmore

Production by James Graves

Typeset by Wyvern Typesetting Ltd

Printed by Scotprint Ltd, Musselburgh

Acknowledgements
The author and publishers would like to thank the following for permission to reproduce illustrations:
Bodleian Library, University of Oxford: p. 94; © British Museum: p. 49; Illustrated London News Picture Library: p. 114; Mansell Collection: pp. 11, 103, 138, 140, 147; Mary Evans Picture Library: pp. 30, 37, 72, 142; Royal Academy of Arts, London: p. 43; Tretyakos Gallery, Moscow/The Bridgeman Art Library: p. 122; University of Bristol Theatre Collection: p. 54. Illustration on p. 116 by M.L. Design.

Thanks are due to the following for permission to reproduce copyright material: George Allen & Unwin, an imprint of Harper-CollinsPublishers for the poem *The Lament of Hsi-Chün* in *170 Chinese Poems* (translated by Arthur Waley, 1919) and the poem *Losing a Slave Girl* from *More Translations from the Chinese* by Po-Chü-I (translated by Arthur Waley, 1919); © Crossley-Holland 1982. Reprinted from *Beowulf*, translated by Kevin Crossley-Holland (1982) by permission of Oxford University Press; Peter Owen Ltd for the extract from *Adventures in the Caucasus* by Alexandre Dumas (translated by A. E. Murch); Joan Rockwell for her translation of *Askenbasken who became Queen*.
Every effort has been made to contact the holders of copyright material if any have been inadvertently overlooked the publishers will be d to make the necessary arrangements at the first opportunity.

CONTENTS

INTRODUCTION

The dark and dangerous has long had a strong influence on readers. This selection, drawn entirely from pre-twentieth century material, contains famous pieces as well as some less well-known ones. They offer thought-provoking and different perspectives and contrasting responses and points of view.

The five sections take various aspects of "Desperate Deeds" and the feelings aroused by them, mixing a wide range of fiction and non-fiction as required by the National Curriculum for English. There is the extravagance of melodrama and the fine subtleties of Emily Dickinson, the daringly imagined and the starkly real. There is sadness and humour, anger and enjoyment. The variety of points of view is sometimes a reminder that there are no simple versions of events: we can compare Russell's and Tennyson's writing based on the events at Balaklava; see the horrors of child labour and then be jolted by the young girl who enjoys what she does; there is the dramatic awfulness of slavery imagined and relived and there is the disconcerting sensitivity of the Chinese slave-owner. Many will know of Frankenstein by name and through films and link it with straightforward horror, but few will know of the complexity of Mary Shelley's creation, seen in the extract where the "monster" explains what he feels and suffers.

Reading this selection is never likely to be a peaceful activity: most pieces are highly dramatic; many need to be performed, as stories well told or dialogue carefully revived by interpreting voices. The pleasures of reading, hearing and sharing the texts here may encourage readers to search out the places that they have come from and the other pleasures that are there.

Sources

Young and Innocent

"The Juniper Tree" is from *Household Tales by the Brothers Grimm*, Everyman Library 1906

"The Wonderful Drama of Punch and Judy" by Papernose Woodensconce Esq. (Robert Brough, 1854) (found in *Punch and Judy – a History* by George Speaight, Studio Vista 1970

"The Story of Little Suck-a-Thumb" is from *Struwwelpeter or Pretty Stories and Funny Pictures* by Dr. Heinrich Hoffman (1848)

"Askenbasken Who Became Queen" (1881) translated by Joan Rockwell in *The Cinderella Story – the origins and variations of the story known as "Cinderella"* by Neil Philip, Penguin Folklore Library 1989

"Poor Little Leo Died This Morning" (1861) by Ellen Buxton in *Journal, 1860–64*, arranged by her granddaughter, Ellen R.C. Creighton, Geoofrey Bles 1967

"Childhood Toys Remembered" by Charles Dickens – from "The Christmas Tree" (1850) in *The Christmas Stories*

Fear and Dread

"Dracula Strikes" from *Dracula* by Bram Stoker (1897)

"The Tell-Tale Heart" by Edgar Allan Poe published in the *Broadway Journal* (1845)

"The Gnat That Mangles Men" – a selection of poems by Emily Dickinson from *The Complete Poems of Emily Dickinson*, edited by Thomas H. Johnson, Faber 1970

"Tied to the Railway Tracks" from *Under The Gaslight* by Augustin Daly (1867)

"Sweeney's Pork Pies" from *The String of Pearls (Sweeney Todd)* by George Dibdin Pitt (1847) (found in *The Golden Age of Melodrama – twelve 19th century melodramas* by Michael Kilgarriff, Wolfe Publishing Ltd 1974)

Chained and Trapped

"The Pain of Slavery" from *The History of Mary Prince – A West Indian Slave – related by herself* (1831)

"Trusting The White Man" from *Oronooko* by Aphra Behn (1868)

"Losing a Slave Girl" by Po Chü-1 (from *More Translations from the Chinese* translated by Arthur Waley, George Allen & Unwin, London 1919)

Letter: "My Dearest George" in *In Darkest England and the Way Out* by William (General) Booth, Salvation Army, London 1890

"The Climbing Boys" extracts from:
The Lady's Magazine 1802; Minutes of Evidence Taken Before the Parliamentary Committee on Employment of Boys in Sweeping of Chimnies, June 23 1817 (in *The Faber Book of Reportage* edited by John Carey, Faber 1987); Evidence to Children's Employment Commission, Parliamentary Papers, 1863 (in *Human Documents of the Victorian Golden Age (1850–75)* by E. Royston Pike, George Allen & Unwin, London 1967); "My Mother Always Brought Me Up To Be A Good Worker" from Mr. White's Report on the Metal Manufacturers of the Birmingham District 3rd Report in Children's Employment Commission 2nd Report (1864) in Parliamentary Papers 1864 volume 22 (in *Human Documents of The Victorian Golden Age (1850–75)*).

"Frankenstein's Creation Asks for Companionship" from *Frankenstein* by Mary Shelley (1818)

"The Lament of Hsi-Chün" (from *170 Chinese Poems* translated by Arthur Waley, George Allen & Unwin 1919)

Death and Glory

"The Killing of the Monster and his Mother" from *Beowulf* retold by Kevin Crossley-Holland, Oxford 1982

"The Bear-Hunt" by Leo Tolstoy from *Twenty-three Tales* translated by Louise and Angus Maude, Oxford University Press 1928

"The Cavalry Action at Balaklava" by William Howard Russell in *The Times* November 14 1854

"The Charge of the Light Brigade" by Alfred Lord Tennyson in Eversley Edition II (1908)

"Fight to the Death" from *Adventures in the Caucasus* by Alexandre Dumas Translated by A. E. Murch, Peter Owen 1962

Crime and Punishment

"Sikes and Nancy" from *Sikes and Nancy and Other Public Readings* by Charles Dickens, edited by Philip Collins, Oxford University Press 1983

"Three Infamous Pirates" from *A General History of the Robberies and Murders of the Most Notorious Pirates* by Captain Charles Johnson (Daniel Defoe) (edited by Manuel Schlonhorn, Dent & Son 1972)

"Improvements in Education" by Joseph Lancaster (1806) (in *Educational Documents 800–1816* by D. W. Sylvester, Methuen 1970)

"The Thief-Taker General" extracts from *It Takes a Thief – the life and times of Jonathan Wild* by Gerald Howson, The Cresset Library, Century Hutchinson 1987

"The Wicked Who Would Do Me Harm" translated by A. Carmichael (in *The Rattle Bag* edited by Heaney and Hughes, Faber 1982)

YOUNG AND INNOCENT

THE BROTHERS GRIMM
(Jacob 1785–1863; Wilhelm 1786–1859)

The Juniper Tree
(collected 1812)

Why is it that bedtime stories for children contain murder, mutilation and cannibalism? The brothers' surname seems exactly right at times and many of the stories, especially in early and "original" versions, may shock you if you only know them from children's books or from Walt Disney's films. They were originally adult folktales and, as in this example, they describe age-old terrors in simple ways, using the safety of magic. This is a fine story which allows a happy ending — only just — to the timeless horrors of child-abuse.

L ONG, LONG AGO, some two thousand years or so, there lived a rich man with a good and beautiful wife. They loved each other dearly, but sorrowed much that they had no children. So greatly did they desire to have one, that the wife prayed for it day and night, but still they remained childless.

In front of the house there was a court, in which grew a juniper tree. One winter's day the wife stood under the tree to peel some apples, and as she was peeling them, she cut her finger, and the blood fell on the snow. "Ah," sighed the woman heavily, "if I had but a child, as red as blood and as white as snow," and as she spoke the words, her heart grew light within her, and it seemed to her that her wish was granted, and she returned to the house feeling glad and comforted. A month passed, and the snow had all disappeared; then another month went by, and all the earth was green. So the months followed one another, and first the trees budded in the woods, and soon the green branches grew thickly inter-twined, and then the blossoms began to fall. Once again the wife stood under the juniper tree, and it was so full of sweet scent that her heart leaped for joy, and she was so overcome with her happiness, that she fell on her knees. Presently the fruit became round and firm, and she was glad and at peace; but when they were fully ripe she picked the berries and ate eagerly of them, and then she grew sad and ill. A little while later

she called her husband, and said to him, weeping, "If I die, bury me under the juniper tree." Then she felt comforted and happy again, and before another month had passed she had a little child, and when she saw that it was as white as snow and as red as blood, her joy was so great that she died.

Her husband buried her under the juniper tree, and wept bitterly for her. By degrees, however, his sorrow grew less, and although at times he still grieved over his loss, he was able to go about as usual, and later on he married again.

He now had a little daughter born to him; the child of his first wife was a boy, who was as red as blood and as white as snow. The mother loved her daughter very much, and when she looked at her and then looked at the boy, it pierced her heart to think that he would always stand in the way of her own child, and she was continually thinking how she could get the whole of the property for her. This evil thought took possession of her more and more, and made her behave very unkindly to the boy. She drove him from place to place with cuffings and buffetings, so that the poor child went about in fear, and had no peace from the time he left school to the time he went back.

One day the little daughter came running to her mother in the store-room, and said, "Mother, give me an apple." "Yes, my child," said the wife, and she gave her a beautiful apple out of the chest; the chest had a very heavy lid and a large iron lock.

"Mother," said the little daughter again, "may not brother have one too?" The mother was angry at this, but she answered, "Yes, when he comes out of school."

Just then she looked out of the window and saw him coming, and it seemed as if an evil spirit entered into her, for she snatched the apple out of her little daughter's hand, and said, "You shall not have one before your brother." She threw the apple into the chest and shut it to. The little boy now came in, and the evil spirit in the wife made her say kindly to him, "My son, will you have an apple?" but she gave him a wicked look. "Mother," said the boy, "how dreadful you look! yes, give me an apple." The thought came to her that she would kill him. "Come with me," she said, and she lifted up the lid of the chest, "take one out for yourself." And as he bent over to do so, the evil spirit urged her, and crash! down went the lid, and off went the little boy's head. Then she was overwhelmed with fear at the thought of what she had done. "If only I can prevent anyone knowing that I did it," she thought. So she went upstairs to her room, and took a white handkerchief out of her top drawer; then she set the boy's head again on his shoulders, and bound it with the handkerchief so that nothing could be seen, and placed him on a chair by the door with an apple in his hand.

Soon after this, little Marleen came up to her mother who was stirring a pot of boiling water over the fire, and said, "Mother, brother is sitting by the door with an apple in his hand, and he looks so pale; and when I asked him to give me the apple, he did not answer, and that frightened me."

"Go to him again," said her mother, "and if he does not answer, give him a box on the ear." So little Marleen went, and said, "Brother, give me that apple," but he did not say a word; then she gave him a box on the ear, and his head rolled off. She was so terrified at this, that she ran crying and screaming to her mother. "Oh!" she said, "I have knocked off brother's head," and then she wept and wept, and nothing would stop her.

"What have you done!" said her mother, "but no one must know about it, so you must keep silence; what is done can't be undone; we will make him into puddings." And she took the little boy and cut him up, made him into puddings, and put him in the pot. But Marleen stood looking on, and wept and wept, and her tears fell into the pot, so that there was no need of salt.

Presently the father came home and sat down to his dinner; he asked, "Where is my son?" The mother said nothing, but gave him a large dish of black pudding, and Marleen still wept without ceasing.

The father again asked, "Where is my son?"

"Oh," answered the wife, "he is gone into the country to his mother's great uncle; he is going to stay there some time."

"What has he gone there for? and he never even said goodbye to me!"

"Well, he likes being there, and he told me he should be away quite six weeks; he is well looked after there."

"I feel very unhappy about it," said the husband, "in case it should not be all right, and he ought to have said goodbye to me." With this he went on with his dinner, and said, "Little Marleen, why do you weep? Brother will soon be back." Then he asked his wife for more pudding, and as he ate, he threw the bones under the table.

Little Marleen went upstairs and took her best silk handkerchief out of her bottom drawer, and in it she wrapped all the bones from under the table and carried them outside, and all the time she did nothing but weep. Then she laid them in the green grass under the juniper tree, and she had no sooner done so, than all her sadness seemed to leave her, and she wept no more. And now the juniper tree began to move, and the branches waved backwards and forwards, first away from one another, and then together again, as it might be someone clapping their hands for joy. After this a mist came round the tree, and in the midst of it there was a burning as of fire, and out of the fire there flew a beautiful bird, that rose high into the air, singing magnificently, and when it could no more be seen, the juniper tree stood there as before, and the silk handkerchief and the bones were gone.

Little Marleen now felt as light-hearted and happy as if her brother were still alive, and she went back to the house and sat down cheerfully to the table and ate.

The bird flew away and alighted on the house of a goldsmith, and began to sing –

> **"My mother killed her little son;**
> **My father grieved when I was gone;**
> **My sister loved me best of all;**
> **She laid her kerchief over me,**
> **And took my bones that they might lie**
> **Underneath the juniper tree.**
> **Kywitt, Kywitt, what a beautiful bird am I!"**

The goldsmith was in his workshop making a gold chain, when he heard the song of the bird on his roof. He thought it so beautiful that he got up and ran out, and as he crossed the threshold he lost one of his slippers. But he ran on into the middle of the street, with a slipper on one foot and a sock on the other; he still had on his apron, and still held the gold chain and the pincers in his hands, and so he stood gazing up at the bird, while the sun came shining brightly down on the street.

"Bird," he said, "how beautifully you sing! sing me that song again."

"Nay," said the bird, "I do not sing twice for nothing. Give me that gold chain, and I will sing it you again."

"Here is the chain, take it," said the goldsmith. "Only sing me that again."

The bird flew down and took the gold chain in his right claw, and then he alighted again in front of the goldsmith and sang –

> **"My mother killed her little son;**
> **My father grieved when I was gone;**
> **My sister loved me best of all;**
> **She laid her kerchief over me,**
> **And took my bones that they might lie**
> **Underneath the juniper tree.**
> **Kywitt, Kywitt, what a beautiful bird am I!"**

Then he flew away, settled on the roof of a shoemaker's house and sang –

> **"My mother killed her little son;**
> **My father grieved when I was gone;**
> **My sister loved me best of all;**

> She laid her kerchief over me,
> And took my bones that they might lie
> Underneath the juniper tree.
> Kywitt, Kywitt, what a beautiful bird am I!"

The shoemaker heard him, and he jumped up and ran out in his shirt-sleeves, and stood looking up at the bird on the roof with his hand over his eyes to keep himself from being blinded by the sun.

"Bird," he said, "how beautifully you sing!" Then he called through the door to his wife; "Wife, come out; here is a bird, come and look at it and hear how beautifully it sings." Then he called his daughter and the children, and then the apprentices, girls and boys, and they all ran up the street to look at the bird, and saw how splendid it was with its red and green feathers, and its neck like burnished gold, and eyes like two bright stars in its head.

"Bird," said the shoemaker, "sing me that song again."

"Nay," answered the bird, "I do not sing twice for nothing; you must give me something."

"Wife," said the man, "go into the garret, on the upper shelf you will see a pair of red shoes; bring them to me." The wife went in and fetched the shoes.

"There, bird," said the shoemaker, "now sing me that song again."

The bird flew down and took the red shoes in his left claw, and then he went back to the roof and sang –

> "My mother killed her little son;
> My father grieved when I was gone;
> My sister loved me best of all;
> She laid her kerchief over me,
> And took my bones that they might lie
> Underneath the juniper tree.
> Kywitt, Kywitt, what a beautiful bird am I!"

When he had finished, he flew away. He had the chain in his right claw and the shoes in his left, and he flew right away to a mill, and the mill went "Click clack, click clack, click clack." Inside the mill were twenty miller's men hewing a stone, and as they went "Hick hack, hick hack, hick hack," the mill went "click clack, click clack, click clack."

The bird settled on a lime-tree in front of the mill and sang –

> "My mother killed her little son;

then one of the men left off,

> **My father grieved when I was gone;**

two more men left off and listened,

> **My sister loved me best of all;**

then four more left off,

> **She laid her kerchief over me,**
> **And took my bones that they might lie**

now there were only eight at work,

> **Underneath the juniper tree.**

and now only one,

> **Kywitt, Kywitt, what a beautiful bird am I!"**

then he too looked up and the last one had left off work.

"Bird," he said, "what a beautiful song that is you sing! Let me hear it too, sing it again."

"Nay," answered the bird, "I do not sing twice for nothing; give me that mill-stone, and I will sing it again."

"If it belonged to me alone," said the man, "you should have it."

"Yes, yes," said the others, "if he will sing again, he can have it."

The bird came down, and all the twenty millers set to and lifted up the stone with a beam; then the bird put his head through the hole and took the stone round his neck like a collar, and flew back with it to the tree and sang –

> **"My mother killed her little son;**
> **My father grieved when I was gone;**
> **My sister loved me best of all;**
> **She laid her kerchief over me,**
> **And took my bones that they might lie**
> **Underneath the juniper tree.**
> **Kywitt, Kywitt, what a beautiful bird am I!"**

And when he had finished his song, he spread his wings, and with the chain in his right claw, the shoes in his left, and the mill-stone round his neck, he flew right away to his father's house.

The father, the mother, and little Marleen were having their dinner.

"How lighthearted I feel," said the father, "so pleased and cheerful."

"And I," said the mother, "I feel so uneasy, as if a heavy thunder-storm were coming."

But little Marleen sat and wept and wept.

Then the bird came flying towards the house and settled on the roof.

"I do feel so happy," said the father, "and how beautifully the sun shines; I feel just as if I were going to see an old friend again."

"Ah!" said the wife, "and I am so full of distress and uneasiness that my teeth chatter, and I feel as if there were a fire in my veins," and she tore open her dress; and all the while little Marleen sat in the corner and wept, and the plate on her knees was wet with her tears.

The bird now flew to the juniper tree and began singing –

"My mother killed her little son;

the mother shut her eyes and her ears, that she might see and hear nothing, but there was a roaring sound in her ears like that of a violent storm, and in her eyes a burning and flashing like lightning –

My father grieved when I was gone;

"Look, mother," said the man, "at the beautiful bird, that is singing so magnificently; and how warm and bright the sun is, and what a delicious scent of spice in the air!"

My sister loved me best of all;

then little Marleen laid her head down on her knees and sobbed.

"I must go outside and see the bird nearer," said the man.

"Ah, do not go," cried his wife, "I feel as if the whole house were in flames."

But the man went out and looked at the bird.

**She laid her kerchief over me,
And took my bones that they might lie
Underneath the juniper tree.
Kywitt, Kywitt, what a beautiful bird am I!"**

With that the bird let fall the gold chain, and it fell just round the man's neck, so that it fitted him exactly.

He went inside, and said, "See, what a splendid bird that is, he has given me this beautiful gold chain, and looks so beautiful himself."

But the wife was in such fear and trouble, that she fell on the floor, and her cap fell from her head.

Then the bird began again –

"My mother killed her little son;

"Ah me!" cried the wife, "if I were but a thousand feet beneath the earth, that I might not hear that song."

My father grieved when I was gone;

then the woman fell down again as if dead.

My sister loved me best of all;

"Well," said little Marleen, "I will go out too and see 'f the bird will give me anything."
So she went out.

> **She laid her kerchief over me,**
> **And took my bones that they might lie**

and he threw down the shoes to her,

> **Underneath the juniper tree.**
> **Kywitt, Kywitt, what a beautiful bird am I!"**

And she now felt quite happy and light-hearted; she put on the shoes and danced and jumped about in them. "I was so miserable," she said, "when I came out, but that has all passed away; that is indeed a splendid bird, and he has given me a pair of red shoes."
The wife sprang up, with her hair standing out from her head like flames of fire. "Then I will go out too," she said, "and see if it will lighten my misery, for I feel as if the world were coming to an end."
But as she crossed the threshold, crash! the bird threw the mill-stone down on her head, and she was crushed to death.
The father and little Marleen heard the sound and ran out, but they only saw mist and flame and fire rising from the spot, and when these had passed, there stood the little brother, and he took the father and little Marleen by the hand; then they all three rejoiced, and went inside together and sat down to their dinners and ate.

"PAPERNOSE WOODENSCONCE ESQ."
(Robert Brough 1828–60)

The Wonderful Drama of Punch and Judy
(1854)

The character of Punch is a very old one stretching back hundreds of years. This script will be instantly recognisable to any who have seen a Punch and Judy performance, which shows just how well he travels through time. With Punch on the left hand, a squeaker in the mouth, a gallery of other characters on the right hand and a real Toby dog, the Punch and Judy performer has a ready play. The scenes can expand or contract but the formula remains with Punch as outrageous as ever, defying the rule of "not in front of the children".

Music. The spirited Proprietor plays 'Pop goes the weasel' or any other popular melody, as much out of tune as possible. Curtain rises.

Punch (*below*) Root-to-to-to-to-too-o-o-it!
Proprietor Now, Mister Punch, I 'ope you're ready.
Punch Shan't be a minute; I'm only putting on my boots.
Prop (*perfectly satisfied with the explanation*) Werry good, sir.
He plays with increased vigour.
Punch (*pops up*) Root-to-to-to-to-it!
Prop Well, Mister Punch, 'ow de do?
Punch How de do?
Prop (*affably*) I am pooty well, Mister Punch, I thank you.
Punch Play us up a bit of a dance.
Prop Cert'ny, Mister Punch.
Music. Punch dances.
Punch Stop! Did you ever see my wife?
Prop (*with dignity*) I never know'd as 'ow you was married, Mister Punch.
Punch Oh! I've got such a splendid wife! (*Calling below*) Judy! – Judy, my darling! – Judy, my duck of several diamonds!

Punch and Judy, drawings by George Cruikshank, 1840s

Enter Judy

Punch   (*admiring his wife*) Ain't she a beauty? There's a nose! Give us a kiss. (*They embrace fondly.*) Now play up.

They dance. At the conclusion, Punch hits his wife on the head with his stick.

Prop   (*severely*) Mister Punch, that's very wrong.

Punch   Haven't I a right to do what I like with my own?

Judy   (*taking stick from him*) In course he has. (*Hitting Punch*) Take that!

Punch   Oh!

Judy   (*hitting him again*) Oh!

Punch   Oh!

Judy   (*hitting him again*) Oh!

Punch   (*taking stick from her, and knocking her out of sight*) Oh! That was to request her to step downstairs to dress the babby. Such a beautiful babby, you've no idea. I'll go and fetch him.

Punch sinks and rises with Baby in his arms.

Punch   (*sings*)   "Hush-a-bye, baby,
                          And sleep while you can;
                          If you live till you're older,
                             You'll grow up a man."

Did you ever see such a beautiful child? and so good?

The Child   (*cries*) Mam-ma-a-a!

Punch   (*thumping him with stick*) Go to sleep, you brat! (*Resumes his song.*)
                      "Hush-a-bye, baby,"–

The Child   (*louder*) Mam-ma-a-a-a!

Punch   (*hitting harder*) Go to sleep!

The Child   (*yells*) Ya-a-a-ah-ah!

Punch   (*hitting him*) Be quiet! Bless him, he's got his father's nose! (*The Child seizes Punch by the nose.*) Murder! Let go! There, go to your mother, if you can't be good.

Punch throws the Child out of window.

Punch   (*sings, drumming with his legs on the front of the stage*)
                      "She's all my fancy painted her,
                         She's lovely, she's divine!"

Enter Judy (*with maternal anxiety depicted on her countenance*).

Judy   Where's the boy?

Punch   The boy?

Judy   Yes.

Punch   What! didn't you catch him?

Judy   Catch him?

Punch   Yes; I threw him out of window. I thought you might be passing.

Judy   Oh! my poor child! Oh! my poor child!

Punch   Why, he was as much mine as yours.

Judy   But you shall pay for it; I'll tear your eyes out.
Punch   Root-to-to-to-to-oo-it!
Kills her at a blow.
Prop   Mr. Punch, you 'ave committed a barbarous and cruel murder, and you must hanswer for it to the laws of your country.
The Beadle enters, brandishing his staff of office.
Beadle   Holloa! holloa! holloa! here I am!
Punch   Holloa! holloa! holloa! and so am I! (*Hits Beadle.*)
Beadle   Do you see my staff, sir?
Punch   Do you feel mine? (*Hits him again.*)
Beadle   (*beating time with his truncheon*) I am the Beadle, Churchwarden, Overseer, Street-keeper, Turncock, Stipendiary Magistrate, and Beadle of the parish!
Punch   Oh! you are the Beagle, Church-warming-pan, Street-sweeper, Turniptop, Stupendiary Magistrate, and Blackbeetle of the parish?
Beadle   I am the Beadle.
Punch   And so am I.
Beadle   You a Beadle?
Punch   Yes.
Beadle   Where's your authority?
Punch   There it is! (*Knocks him down.*)
Beadle   (*rising*) Mr. Punch, you are an ugly ill-bred fellow.
Punch   And so are you.
Beadle   Take your nose out of my face, sir.
Punch   Take your face out of my nose, sir.
Beadle   Pooh!
Punch   Pooh! (*Hits him.*)
Beadle   (*appealing to the Proprietor*) Young man, you are a witness that he has committed an aggravated assault on the majesty of the law.
Punch   Oh! he'd swear anything.
Prop   (*in a reconciling tone*) Don't take no notice of what he says.
Punch   For he'd swear through a brick.
Beadle   It's a conspiracy; I can see through it.
Prop   Through what?
Punch   Through a brick.
Beadle   This mustn't go on, Mr. Punch; I am under the necessity of taking you up.
Punch   And I am under the necessity of knocking you down.
The Beadle falls a lifeless corpse.
Punch   (*in ecstasies*) Roo-to-to-to-to-it! . . .

Punch exults over his successful crimes in a heartless manner, by singing a fragment of a popular melody, and drumming with his heels upon the front of the stage.

Mysterious music, announcing the appearance of the Gho-o-o-o-ost!! who rises and places its unearthly hands upon the bodies of Punch's victims in an awful and imposing manner. The bodies rise slowly.

Punch (*in the same hardened manner, as yet unconscious of the approaching terrors*)

"Rum ti tum ti iddity um.
Pop goes"–

Ghost Boo-o-o-o-oh!
Punch (*frightened*) A-a-a-a-ah!
He kicks frantically, and is supposed to turn deadly pale.
Ghost Boo-o-o-o-oh!
Punch A-a-a-a-ah! (*He trembles like a leaf.*)
Ghost Boo-o-o-o-oh!!
Punch faints. The Ghost and bodies disappear. Punch, by spasmodic convulsions, expresses that the terrors of a guilty conscience, added to the excesses of an irregular course of life, have brought on an intermittent fever.
Punch (*feebly*) I'm very ill: fetch a Doctor.
The Doctor rises.
Doctor Somebody called for a Doctor. Why, I declare it's my old friend Punch. What's the matter with him? (*feeling the patient's pulse*) Fourteen–fifteen–nineteen–six. The man is not dead – almost, quite. Punch, *are* you dead?
Punch (*starting up and hitting him*) Yes.
He relapses into insensibility.
Doctor Mr. Punch, there's no believing you; I don't believe you are dead.
Punch (*hitting him as before*) Yes, I am.
Doctor I tell you what, Punch, I must go and fetch you some physic. (*Exit.*)
Punch (*rising*) A pretty Doctor, to come without physic.
Re-enter Doctor, with cudgel. Punch relapses as before.
Doctor Now, Punch, *are* you dead? No reply! (*Thrashing him.*) Physic! physic! physic!
The mixture as before is repeated each time.
Punch (*reviving under the influence of the dose*) What sort of physic do you call that, Doctor?
Doctor Stick-liquorice! stick-liquorice! stick-liquorice!
The mixture as before, repeated each time.
Punch Stop, Doctor! give me the bottle in my own hands. (*Taking stick from him, and thrashing him with it.*) Physic! physic! physic! (*Doctor yells.*) What a simple Doctor! doesn't like his own physic! Stick-liquorice! stick-liquorice! stick-liquorice!

Doctor (*calling out*) Punch, pay me my fee, and let me go.

Punch What's your fee?

Doctor A guinea.

Punch Give me change out of a fourpenny-bit.

Doctor But a guinea's twenty-one shillings.

Punch Stop! let me feel for my purse. (*Takes up stick and hits Doctor.*) One! two! three! four! Stop! that was a bad one; I'll give you another. Four! five! six!

Hits Doctor twenty-one times. Then looks at him. He is motionless.

Punch Root-to-to-to-to-it! Settled! . . .

Toby rises, barking. Punch embraces him.

Punch There's a beautiful dog! . . . he's so fond of me. Poor little fellow! Toby, ain't you fond of your master?

Toby snaps.

Punch Oh, my nose!

Prop Mr. Punch, you don't conciliate the hanimal properly; you should promise him something nice for supper.

Punch Toby, you shall have a pail of water and a broomstick for supper. (*Toby snaps again.*) I'll knock your brains out.

Prop Don't go to 'urt the dog, Mr. Punch.

Punch I will.

Prop Don't!

Punch I'll knock his brains out, and cut his throat!

Prop How? with your stick?

Punch I will! So here goes. One! two! (*Jones, a respectable tradesman, Toby's former master, rises, and receives the blow intended for Toby.*) Three!

Jones Murder! (*Rubbing his head, to Punch*) I shall make you pay for my head, sir!

Punch And I shall make you pay for my stick, sir!

Jones I haven't broken your stick.

Punch And I haven't broken your head.

Jones You have, sir!

Punch Then it was cracked before.

Jones (*seeing Toby*) Why, that's my dog Toby! Toby, old friend, how are you?

Toby Bow, wow, wow!

Punch He isn't your dog.

Jones He is!

Punch He isn't!

Jones He is! A fortnight ago I lost him.

Punch And a fortnight ago I found him.

Jones We'll see if the dog belongs to you, Mr. Punch. You shall go up to him, and say, "Toby, poor little fellow, how are you?"

Punch   Oh! I'm to go up to him, and say, "Toby, poor little fellow, how are you?"

Jones   Yes.

Punch   Very good.

Punch   (*to Jones*) We'll soon see. (*Goes up to Toby.*) "Toby, poor little fellow, how are you?"

Toby snaps at Punch's nose.

Jones   There! you see!

Punch   What?

Jones   That shows the dog's mine.

Punch   No; it shows he's mine.

Jones   Then if he's yours, why does he bite you?

Punch   Because he likes me.

Jones   Pooh! nonsense! We'll soon settle which of us the dog belongs to, Mr. Punch. We'll fight for him. I'll have the dog to back me up. Toby, I'm going to fight for your liberty. If Punch knocks me down, you pick me up; if Punch wallops me, you wallop him.

Punch   But I'm not going to fight three or four of you.

Jones   The dog is only going to back me up.

Punch   Then somebody must back me up. (*To Proprietor*) Will you back me up, sir?

Prop   (*always willing to oblige*) Cert'ny, Mr. Punch.

They take places for a fight.

Prop   Now, you don't begin till I say "time". (*Punch knocks Jones down.*) Mr. Punch, that wasn't fair.

Punch   Why, you said "time".

Prop   I didn't.

Punch   What did you say, then?

Prop   I said, "You don't begin till I say 'time'."

Punch   There! you said it again. (*Knocks Jones down again.*)

Jones   Toby, I'm down! back me up. (*Toby flies at Punch.*)

Toby   G-r-r-r-r-r-r! (*Bites Punch.*)

Punch   It isn't fair; he didn't say "time".

Jones   At him again, Toby! Good dog!

Toby   G-r-r-r-row-wow! (*Bites again.*)

Punch   Murder! I say, sir, please to call him off!

Prop   Mr. Punch, you must wait till I say "time".

Toby attacks Punch furiously, defending his former Master.

Jones   Perhaps, Mr. Punch, you'll own he's my dog now?

Punch   No, I won't.

Jones   Then anything to please you; I'll tell you what we'll do.

Punch   What?

Jones   We'll toss for him.

Punch   Very well.

Jones   You cry.

Punch   Head! (*Tosses*)

Jones   Tail! It's a tail. Come along, Toby; you're mine.

Punch   He isn't! he's mine.

Jones   I cried tail.

Punch   Then take his tail! I cried head; and you shan't have that!

Jones   I'll have my half.

Punch   And I'll have mine.

They pull Toby between them. The struggle lasts for some time, during which Toby sides with his former Master, by whom he is eventually carried off in triumph.

Punch   (*calling after them*)   I wouldn't have him as a gift; he's got the distemper!

A lapse of time is supposed to have occurred. Punch is in prison, condemned to death for his numerous crimes.

Punch   Oh, dear! I'm in the coal-hole!

Prop   No, Mr. Punch; you are in prison!

Punch   What for?

Prop   For having broken the laws of your country.

Punch   Why, I never touched 'em.

Prop   At any rate, Mr. Punch, you will be hanged.

Punch   Hanged? Oh, dear! oh, dear!

Prop   Yes; and I hope it will be a lesson to you.

Punch   Oh, my poor wife and sixteen small children! all of 'em twins! and the oldest only two years and a half old! B-r-r-r-r!

Punch weeps. The Hangman rises, and erects the gallows.

Hangman   Now, Punch, you are ordered for instant execution.

Punch   What's that?

Hangman   You are to be hanged by the neck till you are dead! dead! dead!

Punch   What! three or four times over?

Hangman   No. Place your head in the centre of the rope there!

Punch   (*wringing his hands*)   Oh, dear! oh, dear!

Hangman   Come, Mr. Punch; Justice can't wait.

Punch   Stop a bit; I haven't made my will.

Hangman   A good thought. We can't think of letting a man die till he's made his will.

Punch   Can't you?

Hangman   Certainly not.

Punch   Then I won't make mine at all.

Hangman   That won't do, Punch. Come, put your head in there.

Punch   (*putting his head under the noose*)   There?

Hangman   No; higher up!

Punch   (*putting his head over*) There?

Hangman   No; lower down!

Punch   There?

Hangman   No, you blockhead; higher!

Punch   Well, I never was hanged before; and I don't know how to do it.

Hangman   Oh! as you never were hanged before, it's but right I should show you the way. Now, Mr. Punch, observe me. In the first place, I put my head in the noose – so!

He puts his head in the noose. Punch watches attentively.

Hangman   (*with his head in the noose*) Now, Mr. Punch, you see my head?

Punch   Yes.

Hangman   Well, when I've got your head in, I pull the end of the rope.

Punch   (*pulling rope a little*) So?

Hangman   Yes, only tighter.

Punch   (*pulling a little more*) So?

Hangman   Tighter than that.

Punch   Very good; I think I know now.

Hangman   Then turn round and bid your friends farewell; and I'll take my head out, and you put yours in.

Punch   Stop a minute. (*Pulls the rope tightly.*) Oee! oee! oee! I understand all about it. Now, oee! oee! oee! (*Pulls the rope, and hangs the Hangman.*) Here's a man tumbled into a ditch, and hung himself up to dry.

Swings Hangman backwards and forwards.

Punch   (*swinging the Hangman's rope*) Oee! oee! oee!

A Horrid Dreadful Personage rises behind Punch, and taps him on the shoulder.

The Horrid Dreadful Personage   You're come for.

Punch   (*alarmed*) Who are you?

The Horrid Dreadful Personage   (*in a terrible voice*) Bogy!

Punch   Oh, dear! what do you want?

Bogy   To carry you off to the land of Bobetty-Shooty, where you will be condemned to the punishment of shaving the monkeys.

Punch   Stop! who were you to ask for?

Bogy   Who? why, Punch, the man who was to be hanged.

Punch   (*pointing to Hangman*) Then there he is!

Bogy   Oh! is that him? Thank you. Good night! (*Carries off Hangman.*)

Punch   (*knocking them both as they go*) Good night!

> (*sings*) "Root-to-to-it! Punch is right, –
> All his enemies put to flight;
> Ladies and gentlemen all, good night
> To the freaks of Punch and Judy!" (*exits*)

The Proprietor   Ladies hand gentlemen, the drama is concluded; and has you like it, so I hopes you'll recommend it. (*Bows gracefully.*)

DR. HEINRICH HOFFMANN (1809–94)

The Story of Little Suck-a-Thumb
(1845)

*This is from **Struwwelpeter**, an astonishing book to present to children. The subtitle of the collection is "Pretty Stories and Funny Pictures" and these are definitely not. The author did not like the coy and moral stories available for his three-year-old son, so he made up his own. What do you think young children would make of this?*

ONE DAY, Mamma said: "Conrad dear.
I must go out and leave you here.
But mind now, Conrad, what I say,
Don't suck your thumb while I'm away.
The great tall tailor always comes
To little boys that suck their thumbs,
And ere they dream what he's about,
He takes his great sharp scissors out
And cuts their thumbs clean off, – and then,
You know, they never grow again."

Mamma had scarcely turn'd her back,
The thumb was in, Alack! Alack!

The door flew open, in he ran,
The great, long, red-legg'd scissor-man.
Oh! children, see! the tailor's come
And caught out little Suck-a-Thumb.
Snip! Snap! Snip! the scissors go;
And Conrad cries out – Oh! Oh! Oh!
Snip! Snap! Snip! They go so fast,
That both his thumbs are off at last.

Mamma comes home; there Conrad stands.
And looks quite sad, and shows his hands, –
"Ah!" said Mamma "I knew he'd come
To naughty little Suck-a-Thumb."

A Danish Cinderella

Askenbasken who became Queen
(Collected 1881)

There are Cinderella-like stories from all over the world and some are very old indeed. The tale takes its roots, like so many, from the French collection of Charles Perrault (1628–1703). This version, translated by Joan Rockwell, makes a fascinating comparison with the one more usually available to us.

THERE WAS A WOMAN who had three daughters, only one of them was a stepdaughter. This girl she treated very ill: she was never allowed to go out with the others on visits, and was always kept at home where she slept in a corner of the kitchen among all the dirt and ashes, and so she was called Askenbasken.

The other two daughters, though, were always dressed up very fine, so that they looked like real young ladies.

There was to be a great ball in the neighbourhood, and the father was to go to the market town and buy fine clothes for the two elder sisters. He asked them what they would have, and they demanded one elegant thing and bit of finery after another. But when he asked Askenbasken what she would have, she said she only wanted a rose-tree, with the roots and all. She wanted to plant it on her mother's grave, but she dare not say so, and her father wondered a good deal why she made this wish, but he bought the rose-tree just the same.

That night when all was still, she stole out of the house and took the tree to her mother's grave where she planted it, and watered it with her tears.

From now on she went there every evening, to see her rose-tree, and it grew so well and was so beautiful that it was a joy to see. But she was even more delighted when she noticed that a white dove came and sat singing in the tree whenever she came; and it sang so sweetly she had never heard anything so rare.

In the meantime the two sisters were getting their finery ready to go to the ball, and they spent all their time arranging it. Askenbasken would

also have liked to go, and she asked if she might. The stepmother didn't quite like to say straight out that she couldn't go, so she flung a plateful of peas into the ashes, and said, if she could gather them up again, each and every one, she could come along to the ball, and they'd find some old rags or other to hang on her.

Anyone would have thought this was an impossible task, and that's what the stepmother thought too. But just as Askenbasken was kneeling and groping for the peas in the ashes, the white dove came flying right against the windowpane under the roof. She went out and let the dove in, and it had a whole troop of birds with it. They all set to work to peck and pick up all the peas, and so they were all collected in a twinkling. But when the girl showed them to her mother, she was so furious that she took a whole apron-full of peas and threw them in the ashes, saying that now Askenbasken could just gather up all those before she came to the ball. Since the ball was to begin that very same afternoon, she was pretty sure not to have Askenbasken dragging along with them.

Soon after this the others drove off, and Askenbasken went up to her mother's grave and cried bitterly. But then the white dove came, and sang that she should cheer up and go home, and there she would find a grand dress she could put on and go to the ball, but she must be sure to get home before the others.

So she got to the ball, and there was no one there more elegant or better dressed than she, and besides that she was a very handsome girl herself. The king himself was there, and he was so pleased with this fair stranger that he danced with her the whole evening. The mother was so insulted because he didn't dance at all with her daughters that she decided to go home far earlier than she had intended. When Askenbasken noticed this, she hurried away from the ball herself and had her fine clothes hidden away before the others got home.

When they did get home, Askenbasken was sly enough to ask them how they had enjoyed the ball. "What's that to do with you, you scarecrow?" they answered; and that was all the reply she got.

The next day they were to go to the ball again. The girls were dressed much finer even than the day before, and off they drove and left Askenbasken to her own devices at home. Away she went to her mother's grave and cried, and immediately the dove came and sat in the rose-tree and sang of the fine clothes that lay at home waiting for her to put them on; but she must be sure to be the first one home.

That evening the king sat with his eyes fixed on the door, for he longed to see the lovely girl from the day before, and had promised himself that she would not slip away from him so easily a second time. In she came, and the king was so much in love that he danced with no one else. But the mother was so envious because her own daughters never got a dance,

even though they were decked out so splendidly, that she decided to go home at once, and wouldn't stay a moment longer at any price. Now Askenbasken too had to hurry away, and she really had to shove the king aside, for he tried to hold her.

But she did get home in time, and hid her fine clothes.

"Well, did you have a good time?" she asked when the others came home. "Mind your own business, Ash-poker," said they.

There was to be a ball again on the third day, which was to be the last day of the festivities. The girls were going to try their luck one more time, so they dressed themselves up and tricked themselves out as fine as ever they could. But the king's eyes were fixed to the door the whole time, waiting for the mysterious beauty, and he had promised himself that he really would hold on to her this evening. When the others had left, Askenbasken went to her mother's grave and wept, and the dove came and sang that the clothes were lying at home and she should go to the ball, but be sure to come home before the others.

And so she went to the ball, and on this evening her clothes were like the purest gold, and she also had golden shoes on, and galoshes to wear as she walked the road, to keep them from getting muddy. Everything went as before, the old woman was insulted and wanted to go home. The king did his best, but the girl tricked him and ran away and though he ran after her he caught nothing but one of her shoes which stuck on the steps as she ran down and flew off her foot.

When the others got home, the clothes were hidden and there she sat in her corner of the kitchen as usual.

"Well, did you have a good time?"

"None of your business, you slipshod wench," said they, and that was all the answer she got.

But now the king had the shoe, and he resolved to ride around the country with it, until he found the girl that it would fit. He travelled here and he travelled there, but there was no one who could wear his shoe. At last he came to the house where they all lived, and he asked the woman if she had any daughters. Yes, she had two. In that case they must try the shoe.

But the eldest could not get it on, for her great toe was too long. Her old mother whispered in her ear, "Cut it off! Better to lose a toe than lose a chance of being queen!" So she went in and took a great knife from the table and cut off her toe. Now she could get the shoe on, and so she was to go home with the king. He rode off with her accordingly, but as they passed the churchyard there sat the dove in the rose-tree and sang:

King, just look at the foot of the bride!
Blood is running down inside!

So he took a look at the shoe, and sure enough, blood was pouring out of it. When he saw that, he rode back and returned the girl. She certainly was not the one he wanted, and he didn't want to be swindled again; but didn't they have another daughter?

Yes, they did have another; and so she was to try on the shoe. But with her the heel was too thick, and she couldn't push her foot all the way down. "That's no great problem," whispered her mother in her ear. "You can always slice a bit off a heel, and it's far better to lose part of a heel than to lose the chance of being queen." So she too went in and took the knife, and sliced a layer off her heel. Now she could get the shoe on, and so she was to go home with the king. But as she rode past the churchyard by his side, the dove sat again in the tree and sang:

> **King, just look at the foot of the bride,**
> **Blood is running down inside!**

And when he looked, sure enough the blood was pouring down, just as the bird sang. So what he did was to ride straight back and say, Now they had fooled him twice, and he had no mind to be swindled again. But didn't they have another daughter? Well, they did as a matter of fact have a sort of simple one, but there was no question of it being her, for she hadn't even been to the ball.

"Let's see her anyway," said the king, "it's just barely possible the shoe might fit her."

So the mother called her and in she came, dirty and sooty and covered with ash, she looked a perfect mess.

"You could at least have brushed the ashes off," said the old woman.

"It doesn't matter," said the king. "No one should be ashamed of the work they do. Do you think you could wear this shoe, little girl?"

"Of course I can," said she, "for it is my own."

"Where did you get it?" says the mother in a rage.

"I see how it is," said the king, "of course she has some fine clothes laid away, like other folk. Go in, my girl, and put on the dress you wore on the first evening of the ball."

So she did, and when she came back the king said, "Now I have found the one I was looking for, and now you must come with me."

Great preparations were made for the wedding. Her sisters were to be the bridesmaids since they were her closest kin. But as they walked into the church the dove flew down and pecked their eyes out, and so they were blind. This was their punishment for being so cruel to their sister.

And ever after the king lived happily with the girl who had been called Askenbasken, but now had to be called queen; for now she was in her rightful place.

ELLEN BUXTON (1848–?)

Poor Little Leo Died This Morning
(1861)

We have Ellen's journal for the four years 1860–64. Child deaths were both much more common than today and frequently written about. Dickens could squeeze enormous emotion from a child death and it was a stock part of melodramas and songs of the time, events dripping with sentimentality. This true diary account by a thirteen year old is very moving and thus very different. It makes you feel the pain and loss as a quietness.

4 Feb. 1861. Lisa's birthday   Poor little Leo died this morning at 4 o'clock, he had been ill since Thursday morning. I will give a description of it:

On Saturday Jan. 26th, we took Leo to Ham House to see Aunt Buxton, with Papa, Mamma, Lisa and I, and the boys, we went on the ice poor little Leo tumbled down and cried but I do not think he hurt himself much, he got onto a chair and I pushed him about for a long time . . .

Sunday 27. Dear Leo quite well except looking very white as he always did. Timmy (who had scaled herself) quite happy in her little bed in the Bow room: Leo went out for a walk in the garden with us before church as usual.

Monday 28. This morning Timmy seemed very dull and low indeed, she would not eat nor play. But dear Leo was quite well. In the afternoon we took Leo with us for a walk to Aunt Barclay's we took Derry without a saddle for him to ride: When we got to the gravel pits we left Arthur Geoffrey and Alfred to try and catch lizards in the little ponds while Lisa Papa Mamma and Myself went on to Aunt Barclay. Leo rode Derry almost all the way there; how little we thought that he would never ride again! When we got to Aunt Barclays we found Mrs. Carter and Mrs. Harrison there with their babies they admired Leo so very much and called him "like a little Angel" he was very much pleased with the beautiful blue and white hyrsenths. As we came home Leo complained of being tired and rather cold when we got in he had forgotten to take off his galoshes in the hall so when he got to the stairs he sat down and said to Lisa, "you can pull them off because they are not very dirty".

Tuesday. Leo came down this morning to reading and sat by Papa on the sofa he looked so lovely by him with his very pale face. Timmie is still very poorly, she looks feverish and is very low indeed. In the afternoon Leo went out into the garden and he was sorry to see all the Barley for the chickens spilt upon the ground so he stayed for a long time picking them up.

Wednesday. Leo quite well . . . In the afternoon Leo went out of door Miss Smith met him and Sarah and Janet at the pond watching the boys skating and sliding, Miss Smith went on but Leo called out to her to stop for him. She took him with her and as they were coming round the garden he found a stick which he said would do for some poor woman.

Jan. 31. This morning Leo had a bad earache he had had it all night and cried a great deal with it, he did not look at all well, poor little boy, but we did not think it was anything. After breakfast Doctor Ansle came we had all been to see Timmie that morning, he told us that she had scarlet Tina, but only slightly: and then we were quite sure that she had had it all Wednesday.

Dr. Ansle told us that dear Leo had it also but so very slightly; he had only a little rash under his arms and legs. That morning at ten o'clock (before Dr. Ansle had come) dear Leo had been sitting with us while we were at lessons and bible reading we gave him a pencil and paper to draw, he drew very nicely and when Lucy brought Arty and I our Codliver oil she said she would go and get dear Leo some orange for to eat while he drew; which he enjoyed very much he looked very pale indeed, all over his face except one little spot on his right cheek, which was very red.

Friday, Feb. 1st. This morning Leo was not very ill, neither was Mamma at all anxious about him, but Emily was much worse than he was, he had hardly any rash. At dinner time Papa took up Emily a choice peice of pheasant with breadsauce and potatoe, but she refused the pheasant and would only eat the breadsauce and potatoe, so Papa took it in to dear Leo which he ate ravenously, it was the last thing he ate that he enjoyed.

Saturday. Today is dear Emily's sixth birthday Leo rather worse he has very bad swellings on his glands and very little rash; in the afternoon he got much worse he could not swallow and hardly spoke and Mamma

says he was in great pain till he died. In the evening she began to be quite anxious about him. Emily is much the same, though she is very ill.

Sunday. Dear Leo very ill indeed Mamma and Papa are very anxious about him . . . Aunt and Uncle Barclay came on their way to meeting and Papa told them how ill Leo was. We did not go to church at all for fear of infection.

Monday Feb. 4. This morning when we went in to Mamma she told us that dear Leo had died in the night; we were all very sorry indeed she told us he had died about 4 o'clock in the morning, and that he had been in great pain before. We all stayed with Papa and Mamma till reading time in their room, then we went down to prayers and Papa read the first part of the XVIIIth chapter of Matthew with the text in it "There angels do always behold the face of my Father". After breakfast Aunt Buxton came and talked with Mamma and Papa, we settled with Miss Smith as usual at 10 o'clock but we did not do regular lessons, Lisa and I went to be with Mamma part of the time, to walk in the garden with her and Aunt Buxton.

6th. This morning Mamma told us that she wanted us to go and see dear Leo before he was put into his little coffin; Lisa Johnney and I went with Papa and Mamma after breakfast; he was lying in the large bed, and he looked so beautiful and so perfectly at rest; but he did not look at all like himself when he was alive, he was so changed I should not have known him I am sure and so exactly like Papa he looked much older than he really was, and so very handsome, his lips were very dark purple nearly black, and he had a sort of yellowish hue all over his face; his hands were under the sheets so we did not see them, there was a handkerchief tied round his face because Mamma said it wanted support. Papa told us to remember his dear face all our life and to look at him intently he did indeed look lovely and just as though he were asleep; because his beautiful brown eyes were shut.

Feb. 7. Today is dear Leos funeral; Cousin John Paterson is coming to bury him. There are to be a great many people all the Aunts and Uncles and cousins are coming . . . At 12 o'clock we began to walk to the churchyard Mamma and Papa went first then came Lisa and I, and then followed all the others, we first went to the churchyard where Cousin John Paterson met us reading some beautiful texts when we went into the church where we read some part of the service, then we went to the little corner in which the grave was dug, by the side of the little twins and Aunt Buxton's little boy. Then we came away and walked home, when we got home Aunt Barclay and everybody else that had come went to Aunt Barclay's and left us all alone.

JAMES WHITCOMB RILEY (1849–1916)

Little Orphant Annie

Riley was enormously popular in his native America during his lifetime and this poem was said to be read wherever there was a schoolroom or a nursery. The character lives on through the comic strip and the film "Annie". The use of dialect may not always be easy to cope with but here the words slip easily into an accent and the whole thing just needs to be performed – and you can tell what audience it needs too.

LITTLE ORPHANT ANNIE's come to our house to stay,
An' wash the cups an' saucers up, an' brush the crumbs away,
An' shoo the chickens off the porch, an' dust the hearth an' sweep,
An' make the fire, an' bake the bread, an' earn her board an' keep:
An' all us other children, when the supper things is done,
We set around the kitchen fire an' has the mostest fun
A-list'nin' to the witch tales 'at Annie tells about,
An' the Gobble-uns 'at gits you
     Ef you
     Don't
      Watch
      Out!

Onc't they was a little boy wouldn't say his pray'rs –
An' when he went to bed 'at night, away up-stairs,
His mammy heerd him holler, an' his daddy heerd him bawl,
An' when they turn't the kivvers down, he wasn't there at all!
An' they seeked him in the rafter-room, an' cubby-hole an' press.
An' seeked him up the chimbly-flue, and every wheres, I guess,
But all they ever found was thist his pants an' roundabout!
An' the Gobble-uns'll git you
     Ef you
     Don't
      Watch
      Out!

An' one time a little girl 'ud allus laugh an' grin,
An' make fun of ever' one an' all her blood an' kin,
An' onc't when they was "company", an' ol' folks was there,
She mocked 'em an' shocked 'em, an' said she didn't care!
An' thist as she kicked her heels, an' turn't to run an' hide,
They was two great big Black Things a-standin' by her side,
An' they snatched her through the ceilin' 'fore she knowed what she's
    about!
An' the Gobble-uns'll git you
        Ef you
          Don't
            Watch
             Out!

An' Little Orphant Annie says, when the blaze is blue,
An' the lampwick splutters, an' the wind goes woo-oo!
An' you hear the crickets quit, an' the moon is gray,
An' the lightnin'-bugs in dew is all squenched away, –
You better mind yer parents, and yer teachers fond and dear,
An' churish them 'at loves you, an' dry the orphant's tear,
An' he'p the pore and needy ones 'at clusters all about,
Er the Gobble-uns'll git you
        Ef you
          Don't
            Watch
             Out!

CHARLES DICKENS (1812–70)

Childhood toys remembered
(from *The Christmas Tree*, 1850)

Dickens's writing about children is always fascinating because he has the sentimental love of childhood while always remembering the fears and darkest moments of childhood helplessness. He writes in this same essay that Little Red Riding Hood was his "first love . . . if I could have married (her) I should have known perfect bliss." And yet look at how he recreates the terrors in these memories of toys.

BEING NOW at home again, and alone, the only person in the house awake, my thoughts are drawn back, by a fascination which I do not care to resist, to my own childhood. I begin to consider, what do we all remember best upon the branches of the Christmas Tree of our own young Christmas days, by which we climbed to real life.

Straight, in the middle of the room, cramped in the freedom of its growth by no encircling walls or soon-reached ceiling, a shadowy tree arises; and, looking up into the dreamy brightness of its top – for I observe in this tree the singular property that it appears to grow downward towards the earth – I look into my youngest Christmas recollections!

All toys at first, I find. Up yonder, among the green holly and red berries, is the Tumbler with his hands in his pockets, who wouldn't lie down, but whenever he was put upon the floor, persisted in rolling his fat body about, until he rolled himself still, and brought those lobster eyes of his to bear upon me – when I affected to laugh very much, but in my heart of hearts was extremely doubtful of him. Close beside him is that infernal snuff-box, out of which there sprang a demoniacal Counsellor in a black gown, with an obnoxious head of hair, and a red cloth mouth, wide open, who was not to be endured on any terms, but could not be put away either; for he used suddenly, in a highly magnified state, to fly out of Mammoth Snuff-boxes in dreams, when least expected. Nor is the frog with cobbler's wax on his tail, far off; for there was no knowing where he wouldn't jump; and when he flew over the candle, and came upon one's hand with that spotted back – red on a green ground – he was horrible. The cardboard lady in a blue-silk skirt, who was stood up against the candlestick to dance, and whom I see on the same branch, was milder, and was beautiful; but I can't say as much for the larger cardboard man, who used to be hung against the wall and pulled by a string; there was a sinister expression in that nose of his; and when he got his legs round his neck (which he very often did), he was ghastly, and not a creature to be alone with.

When did that dreadful Mask first look at me? Who put it on, and why was I so frightened that the sight of it is an era in my life? It is not a hideous visage in itself; it is even meant to be droll; why then were its stolid features so intolerable? Surely not because it hid the wearer's face. An apron would have done as much; and though I should have preferred even the apron away, it would not have been absolutely insupportable, like the mask. Was it the immovability of the mask? The doll's face was immovable, but I was not afraid of *her*. Perhaps that fixed and set change coming over a real face, infused into my quickened heart some remote suggestion and dread of the universal change that is to come on every face, and make it still? Nothing reconciled me to it. No drummers, from whom proceeded a melancholy chirping on the turning of a handle; no regiment of soldiers, with a mute band, taken out of a box, and fitted, one by one, upon a stiff and lazy little set of lazy-tongs; no old woman, made of wires and a brown-paper composition, cutting up a pie for two small children; could give me a permanent comfort, for a long time. Nor was it any satisfaction to be shown the Mask, and see that it was made of paper, or to have it locked up and be assured that no one wore it. The mere recollection of that fixed face, the mere knowledge of its existence anywhere, was sufficient to awake me in the night all perspiration and horror, with, "O I know it's coming! O the mask!"

FEAR AND DREAD

BRAM STOKER (1847–1912)

Dracula strikes
(from *Dracula*, 1897)

The character and elements of this classic horror story have a life in films well beyond the book. Stoker didn't invent Dracula, but he did create the character and plot which countless other stories and films have drawn upon. Don't assume that the novel is as mindless as its imitations – it remains a wonderfully exciting and appalling story. This extract tries to show why.

HE TURNED the handle as he spoke, but the door did not yield. We threw ourselves against it; with a crash it burst open, and we almost fell headlong into the room. The Professor did actually fall, and I saw across him as he gathered himself up from hands and knees. What I saw appalled me. I felt my hair rise like bristles on the back of my neck, and my heart seemed to stand still.

The moonlight was so bright that through the thick yellow blind the room was light enough to see. On the bed beside the window lay Jonathan Harker, his face flushed and breathing heavily as though in a stupor. Kneeling on the near edge of the bed facing outwards was the white-clad figure of his wife. By her side stood a tall, thin man, clad in black. His face was turned from us, but the instant we saw we all recognised the Count – in every way, even to the scar on his forehead. With his left hand he held both Mrs. Harker's hands, keeping them away with her arms at full tension; his right hand gripped her by the back of the neck, forcing her face down on his bosom. Her white night-dress was smeared with blood, and a thin stream trickled down the man's bare breast which was shown by his torn-open dress. The attitude of the two had a terrible resemblance to a child forcing a kitten's nose into a saucer of milk to compel it to drink. As we burst into the room, the Count turned his face, and the hellish look that I had heard described seemed to leap into it. His eyes flamed red with devilish passion; the great nostrils of the white aquiline nose opened wide and quivered at the edge; and the white sharp teeth, behind the full lips of the blood dripping mouth, champed together like those of a wild beast. With a wrench, which threw his victim back upon the bed as though hurled from a height, he turned and sprang at us. But by this time the Professor had gained his feet, and was holding towards him the envelope which contained the Sacred Wafer. The Count suddenly stopped, just as poor Lucy had done outside the tomb, and cowered back. Further and further back he cowered, as we, lifting our crucifixes, advanced. The moonlight suddenly failed, as a great black cloud sailed across the sky; and when the gaslight sprang up under Quincey's match, we saw nothing but a faint vapour. This, as we looked, trailed under the door, which with the recoil from its bursting open, had swung back to its old position. Van Helsing, Art, and I moved forward to Mrs. Harker, who by this time had drawn her breath and with it had given a scream so wild, so ear-piercing, so despairing that it seems to me now that it will ring in my ears till my dying day. For a few seconds she lay in her helpless attitude and disarray. Her face was ghastly, with a pallor which was accentuated by the blood which smeared her lips and cheeks and chin; from her throat trickled a thin stream of blood. Her eyes were mad with terror. Then she put before her face her poor crushed hands, which bore on their whiteness the red mark of the Count's terrible grip, and from behind them came a low desolate wail which made the terrible scream seem only the quick expression of an endless grief. Van Helsing stepped forward and drew the coverlet gently over her body . . .

For a space of perhaps a couple of minutes there was silence, and I could fancy that I could hear the sound of our hearts beating; then Van Helsing said, placing his hand very tenderly on Mrs. Harker's head:

"And now, Madam Mina – poor, dear, dear Madam Mina – tell us exactly what happened. God knows that I do not want that you be pained; but it is need that we know all. For now more than ever has all work to be done quick and sharp, and in deadly earnest. The day is close to us that must end all, if it may so be; and now is the chance that we may live and learn."

The poor, dear lady shivered, and I could see the tension of her nerves as she clasped her husband closer to her and bent her head lower and lower still on his breast. Then she raised her head proudly, and held out one hand to Van Helsing who took it in his, and, after stooping and kissing it reverently, held it fast. The other hand was locked in that of her husband, who held his other arm thrown round her protectingly. After a pause in which she was evidently ordering her thoughts, she began:

"I took the sleeping draught which you had so kindly given me, but for a long time it did not act. I seemed to become more wakeful, and myriads of horrible fancies began to crowd in upon my mind – all of

them connected with death, and vampires; with blood, and pain, and trouble." Her husband involuntarily groaned as she turned to him and said lovingly: "Do not fret, dear. You must be brave and strong, and help me through the horrible task. If you only knew what an effort it is to me to tell of this fearful thing at all, you would understand how much I need your help. Well, I saw I must try to help the medicine to its work with my will, if it was to do me any good, so I resolutely set myself to sleep. Sure enough sleep must soon have come to me, for I remember no more. Jonathan coming in had not waked me, for he lay by my side when next I remember. There was in the room the same thin white mist that I had before noticed. But I forget now if you know of this; you will find it in my diary which I shall show you later. I felt the same vague terror which had come to me before, and the same sense of some presence. I turned to wake Jonathan, but found that he slept so soundly that it seemed as if it was he who had taken the sleeping draught, and not I. I tried, but I could not wake him. This caused me a great fear, and I looked around terrified. Then indeed, my heart sank within me: beside the bed, as if he had stepped out of the mist – or rather as if the mist had turned into his figure, for it had entirely disappeared – stood a tall, thin man, all in black. I knew him at once from the descriptions of the others. The waxen face; the high aquiline nose, on which the light fell in a thin white line; the parted red lips, with the sharp white teeth showing between; and the red eyes that I had seemed to see in the sunset on the windows of St. Mary's Church at Whitby. I knew, too, the red scar on his forehead where Jonathan had struck him. For an instant my heart stood still, and I would have screamed out, only that I was paralysed. In the pause he spoke in a sort of keen, cutting whisper, pointing as he spoke to Jonathan:

" 'Silence! If you make a sound I shall take him and dash his brains out before your very eyes.' I was appalled and was too bewildered to do or say anything. With a mocking smile, he placed one hand upon my shoulder and, holding me tight, bared my throat with the other, saying as he did so: 'First, a little refreshment to reward my exertions. You may as well be quiet; it is not the first time, or the second, that your veins have appeased my thirst!' I was bewildered, and, strangely enough, I did not want to hinder him. I suppose it is a part of the horrible curse that such is, when his touch is on his victim. And oh, my God, my God, pity me! He placed his reeking lips upon my throat!" Her husband groaned again. She clasped his hand harder, and looked at him pity-ingly, as if he were the injured one, and went on:

"I felt my strength fading away, and I was in a half swoon. How long this horrible thing lasted I know not; but it seemed that a long time must have passed before he took his foul, awful, sneering mouth away. I saw it

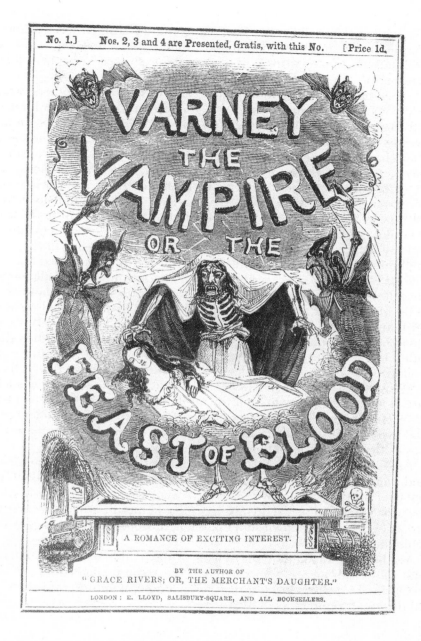

This first vampire novel in English, by Thomas Rymer was very long, appearing like a soap opera in 109 weekly parts from 1845–47.

drip with the fresh blood!" The remembrance seemed for a while to overpower her, and she drooped and would have sunk down but for her husband's sustaining arm. With a great effort she recovered herself and went on:

"Then he spoke to me mockingly, 'And so you, like the others, would play your brains against mine. You would help these men to hunt me and frustrate me in my designs! You know now, and they know in part already, and will know in full before long, what it is to cross my path. They should have kept their energies for use closer to home. Whilst they played wits against me – against me who commanded nations, and intrigued for them, and fought for them, hundreds of years before they were born – I was countermining them. And you, their best beloved one, are now to me, flesh of my flesh; blood of my blood; kin of my kin; my bountiful wine-press for a while; and shall be later on my companion and my helper. You shall be avenged in turn; for not one of them but shall minister to your needs. But as yet you are to be punished for what you have done. You have aided in thwarting me; now you shall come to my call. When my brain says "Come!" to you, you shall cross land or sea to do my bidding; and to that end this!' With that he pulled open his shirt, and with his long sharp nails opened a vein in his breast. When the blood began to spurt out, he took my hands in one of his, holding them tight, and with the other seized my neck and pressed my mouth to the wound, so that I must either suffocate or swallow some of the – Oh my God! my God! what have I done? What have I done to deserve such a fate, I who have tried to walk in meekness and righteousness all my days. God pity me! Look down on a poor soul in worse than mortal peril; and in mercy pity those to whom she is dear!" Then she began to rub her lips as though to cleanse them from pollution.

As she was telling her terrible story, the eastern sky began to quicken, and everything became more and more clear. Harker was still and quiet; but over his face, as the awful narrative went on, came a grey look which deepened and deepened in the morning light, till when the first red streak of the coming dawn shot up, the flesh stood darkly out against the whitening hair.

We have arranged that one of us is to stay within call of the unhappy pair till we can meet together and arrange about taking action.

Of this I am sure: the sun rises today on no more miserable house in all the great round of its daily course.

EDGAR ALLAN POE (1809–49)

The Tell-Tale Heart
(1845)

Poe's stories can be chilling, haunting and fascinating as he shows us terrors and the source of nightmares. "The Pit and the Pendulum", "The Black Cat" and "The Fall of the House of Usher" are just a few of the others which, like this story, show Poe's skill at creating horror.

TRUE! – NERVOUS – very, very dreadfully nervous I had been and am; but why *will* you say that I am mad? The disease had sharpened my senses – not destroyed – not dulled them. Above all was the sense of hearing acute. I heard all things in the heaven and in the earth. I heard many things in hell. How, then, am I mad? Hearken! and observe how healthily – how calmly I can tell you the whole story.

It is impossible to say how first the idea entered my brain; but once conceived, it haunted me day and night. Object there was none. Passion there was none. I loved the old man. He had never wronged me. He had never given me insult. For his gold I had no desire. I think it was his eye! yes, it was this! He had the eye of a vulture – a pale blue eye, with a film over it. Whenever it fell upon me, my blood ran cold; and so by degrees – very gradually – I made up my mind to take the life of the old man, and thus rid myself of the eye forever.

Now this is the point. You fancy me mad. Madmen know nothing. But you should have seen *me*. You should have seen how wisely I proceeded – with what caution – with what foresight – with what dissimulation I went to work! I was never kinder to the old man than during the whole week before I killed him. And every night, about midnight, I turned the latch of his door and opened it – oh so gently! And then, when I had made an opening sufficient for my head, I put in a dark lantern, all closed, closed, so that no light shone out, and then I thrust in my head. Oh, you would have laughed to see how cunningly I thrust it in! I moved it slowly – very, very slowly, so that I might not disturb the old man's sleep. It took me an hour to place my whole head within the opening so far that I could see him as he lay upon his bed. Ha! – would a madman have been so wise as this? And then, when my head was well in the room, I undid the lantern cautiously – oh, so cautiously – cautiously (for the hinges creaked) – I undid it just so much that a single thin ray fell upon the vulture eye. And this I did for seven long nights – every night just at midnight – but I found the eye always closed; and so it was impossible to do the work; for it was not the old man who vexed me, but his Evil Eye. And every morning, when the day broke, I went boldly into the chamber, and spoke courageously to him, calling him by name in a hearty tone, and inquiring how he had passed the night. So you see he would have been a very profound old man, indeed, to suspect that every night, just at twelve, I looked in upon him while he slept.

Upon the eighth night I was more than usually cautious in opening the door. A watch's minute hand moves more quickly than did mine. Never before that night, had I *felt* the extent of my own powers – of my sagacity. I could scarcely contain my feelings of triumph. To think that there I was, opening the door, little by little, and he not even to dream of my secret deeds or thoughts. I fairly chuckled at the idea; and perhaps he heard me; for he moved on the bed suddenly, as if startled. Now you may think that I drew back – but no. His room was as black as pitch with the thick darkness, (for the shutters were close fastened, through fear of robbers,) and so I knew that he could not see the opening of the door, and I kept pushing it on steadily, steadily.

I had my head in, and was about to open the lantern, when my thumb slipped upon the tin fastening, and the old man sprang up in bed, crying out – "Who's there?"

I kept quite still and said nothing. For a whole hour I did not move a muscle, and in the meantime I did not hear him lie down. He was still sitting up in the bed listening; – just as I have done, night after night, hearkening to the death watches in the wall.

Presently I heard a slight groan, and I knew it was the groan of mortal terror. It was not a groan of pain or of grief – oh, no! – it was the low stifled sound that arises from the bottom of the soul when overcharged with awe. I knew the sound well. Many a night, just at midnight, when all the world slept, it has welled up from my own bosom, deepening, with its dreadful echo, the terrors that distracted me. I say I knew it well. I knew what the old man felt, and pitied him, although I chuckled at heart. I knew that he had been lying awake ever since the first slight noise, when he had turned in the bed. His fears had been ever since growing upon him. He had been trying to fancy them causeless, but could not. He had been saying to himself – "It is nothing but the wind in the chimney – it is only a mouse crossing the floor," or "it is merely a cricket which has made a single chirp." Yes, he had been trying to comfort himself with these suppositions: but he had found all in vain. *All in vain*; because Death, in approaching him had stalked with his black shadow before him, and enveloped the victim. And it was the mournful influence of the unperceived shadow that caused him to feel – although he neither saw nor heard – to *feel* the presence of my head within the room.

When I had waited a long time, very patiently, without hearing him lie down, I resolved to open a little – a very, very little crevice in the lantern. So I opened it – you cannot imagine how stealthily, stealthily – until, at length a simple dim ray, like the thread of the spider, shot from out the crevice and fell full upon the vulture eye.

It was open – wide, wide open – and I grew furious as I gazed upon it. I saw it with perfect distinctness – all a dull blue, with a hideous veil over it that chilled the very marrow in my bones; but I could see nothing else of the old man's face or person: for I had directed the ray as if by instinct, precisely upon the damned spot.

And have I not told you that what you mistake for madness is but over acuteness of the senses? – now, I say, there came to my ears a low, dull, quick sound, such as a watch makes when enveloped in cotton. I knew *that* sound well, too. It was the beating of the old man's heart. It increased my fury, as the beating of a drum stimulates the soldier into courage.

But even yet I refrained and kept still. I scarcely breathed. I held the lantern motionless. I tried as steadily as I could to maintain the ray upon the eye. Meantime the hellish tattoo of the heart increased. It grew quicker and quicker, and louder and louder every instant. The old man's terror *must* have been extreme! It grew louder, I say, louder every moment! – do you mark me well? I have told you that I am nervous: so I am. And now at the dead hour of the night, amid the dreadful silence of that old house, so strange a noise as this excited me to uncontrollable terror. Yet, for some minutes longer I refrained and stood still. But the beating grew louder, louder! I thought the heart must burst. And now a new anxiety seized me – the sound would be heard by a neighbour! The old man's hour had come! With a loud yell, I threw open the lantern and leaped into the room. He shrieked once – once only. In an instant I dragged him to the floor, and pulled the heavy bed over him. I then smiled gaily, to find the deed so far done. But, for many minutes, the heart beat on with a muffled sound. This, however, did not vex me; it would not be heard through the wall. At length it ceased. The old man was dead. I removed the bed and examined the corpse. Yes, he was stone, stone dead. I placed my hand upon the heart and held it there many minutes. There was no pulsation. He was stone dead. His eye would trouble me no more.

If still you think me mad, you will think so no longer when I describe the wise precautions I took for the concealment of the body. The night waned, and I worked hastily, but in silence. First of all I dismembered the corpse. I cut off the head and the arms and the legs.

I then took up three planks from the flooring of the chamber, and deposited all between the scantlings*. I then replaced the boards so cleverly, so cunningly, that no human eye – not even *his* – could have detected any thing wrong. There was nothing to wash out – no stain of any kind – no blood-spot whatever. I had been too wary for that. A tub had caught all – ha! ha!

When I had made an end of these labours, it was four o'clock – still dark as midnight. As the bell sounded the hour, there came a knocking at the street door. I went down to open it with a light heart, – for what had I *now* to fear? There entered three men, who introduced themselves, with perfect suavity, as officers of the police. A shriek had been heard by a neighbour during the night; suspicion of foul play had been aroused; information had been lodged at the police office, and they (the officers) had been deputed to search the premises.

I smiled, – for *what* had I to fear? I bade the gentlemen welcome. The shriek, I said, was my own in a dream. The old man, I mentioned, was absent in the country. I took my visitors all over the house. I bade them search – search *well*. I led them, at length, to *his* chamber. I showed them his treasures, secure, undisturbed. In the enthusiasm of my confidence, I brought chairs into the room, and desired them *here* to rest from their fatigues, while I myself, in the wild audacity of my perfect triumph, placed my own seat upon the very spot beneath which reposed the corpse of the victim.

The officers were satisfied. My *manner* had convinced them. I was singularly at ease. They sat, and while I answered cheerily, they chatted of familiar things. But, ere long, I felt myself getting pale and wished them gone. My head ached, and I fancied a ringing in my ears: but still they sat and still chatted. The ringing became more distinct: – it continued and became more distinct: I talked more freely to get rid of the feeling: but it continued and gained definiteness – until, at length, I found that the noise was *not* within my ears.

No doubt I now grew *very* pale; – but I talked more fluently, and with a heightened voice. Yet the sound increased – and what could I do? It was *a low, dull, quick sound – much such a sound as a watch makes when enveloped in cotton*. I gasped for breath – and yet the officers heard it not. I talked more quickly – more vehemently; but the noise steadily increased. I arose and argued about trifles, in a high key and with violent gesticulations; but the noise steadily increased. Why would they not be gone? I

* scantlings: timber beams on which the floorboards rested.

paced the floor to and fro with heavy strides, as if excited to fury by the observations of the men – but the noise steadily increased. Oh God! what could I do? I foamed – I raved – I swore! I swung the chair upon which I had been sitting, and grated it upon the boards, but the noise arose over all and continually increased. It grew louder – louder – *louder*! And still the men chatted pleasantly, and smiled. Was it possible they heard not? Almighty God! – no, no! They heard! – they suspected! – they *knew*! – they were making a mockery of my horror! – this I thought, and this I think. But anything was better than this agony! Anything was more tolerable than this derision! I could bear those hypocritical smiles no longer! I felt that I must scream or die! and now – again! – hark! louder! louder! louder! *louder!*

"Villains!" I shrieked, "dissemble no more! I admit the deed! – tear up the planks! here, here! – it is the beating of his hideous heart!"

"The Night Alarm" by Charles West, 1876

EMILY DICKINSON (1830–86)

"The Gnat that Mangles Men"

A selection of poems of suspense

Only four of Emily Dickinson's poems were published in her lifetime although she wrote about 1800. The way she writes is peculiar to her but try reading them aloud, using her strange punctuation to guide your voice, not your eyes. The poems and individual lines and phrases in them are like telegrams, often startling crisp "messages" with words kept to a minimum. She isn't especially known for being like Stoker or Poe but look at the way she catches the grip of suspense — "Seesawing" "On a Hair's result", or the feeling of terror — "Zero at the Bone".

ONE NEED not be a Chamber – to
be Haunted –
One need not be a House –
The Brain has Corridors–surpassing
Material Place –

Far safer, of a Midnight Meeting
External Ghost
Than its interior Confronting –
That Cooler Host.

Far safer, through an Abbey gallop,
The Stones a'chase –
Than Unarmed, one's a'self encounter –
In lonesome Place –

Ourself behind ourself, concealed –
Should startle most –
Assassin hid in our Apartment
Be Horror's least.

The Body – borrows a Revolver –
He bolts the Door –
O'erlooking a superior spectre –
Or More –

Wonder – is not precisely Knowing
And not precisely Knowing not –
A beautiful but bleak condition
He has not lived who has not felt –

Suspense – is his maturer Sister –
Whether Adult Delight is Pain
Or of itself a new misgiving –
This is the Gnat that mangles men –

Robbed by Death – but that was easy –
To the failing Eye
I could hold the latest Glowing –
Robbed by Liberty

For Her Jugular Defences –
This, too, I endured –
Hint of Glory – it afforded –
For the Brave Beloved –

Fraud of Distance – Fraud of Danger,
Fraud of Death – to bear –
It is Bounty – to Suspense's
Vague Calamity –

Staking our entire Possession
On a Hair's result –
Then – Seesawing – coolly – on it –
Trying if it split –

Suspense – is Hostiler than Death –
Death – tho'soever Broad,
Is just Death, and cannot increase –
Suspense – does not conclude –

But perishes – to live anew –
But just anew to die –
Annihilation – plated fresh
With Immortality –

I KNOW some lonely Houses off the Road
A Robber'd like the look of –
Wooden barred,
And Windows hanging low,
Inviting to –
A Portico,
Where two could creep –
One – hand the Tools –
The other peep –
To make sure All's Asleep –
Old fashioned eyes –
Not easy to surprise!

How orderly the Kitchen'd look, by night,
With just a Clock –
But they could gag the Tick –
And Mice won't bark –
And so the Walls – don't tell –
None – will –

A pair of Spectacles ajar just stir –
An Almanac's aware –
Was it the Mat – winked,
Or a Nervous Star?
The Moon – slides down the stair,
To see who's there!

There's plunder – where –
Tankard, or Spoon –
Earring – or Stone –
A Watch – Some Ancient Brooch
To match the Grandmama –
Staid sleeping – there –

Day – rattles – too
Stealth's – slow –
The Sun has got as far
As the third Sycamore –
Screams Chanticleer
"Who's there"?

And Echoes – Trains away,
Sneer – "Where"!
While the old Couple, just astir,
Fancy the Sunrise – left the door ajar!

A NARROW FELLOW in the Grass
Occasionally rides –
You may have met Him – did you not
His notice sudden is –

The Grass divides as with a Comb –
A spotted shaft is seen –
And then it closes at your feet
And opens further on –
He likes a Boggy Acre
A Floor too cool for Corn –
Yet when a Boy, and Barefoot –
I more than once at Noon
Have passed, I thought, a Whip lash
Unbraiding in the Sun
When stooping to secure it
It wrinkled, and was gone –

Several of Nature's People
I know, and they know me –
I feel for them a transport
Of cordiality –

But never met this Fellow
Attended, or alone
Without a tighter breathing
And Zero at the Bone –

THE Soul's distinct connection
With immortality
Is best disclosed by Danger
Or quick Calamity –

As Lightning on a Landscape
Exhibits Sheets of Place –
Not yet suspected – but for Flash –
And Click – and Suddenness.

THOMAS HOOD (1799-1845)

Mary's Ghost – a pathetic ballad

Hood's poems are often in anthologies and he is worth searching out – for his stories too. This poem shouldn't be funny; the events it describes are awful and record what happened to many dead bodies when the "resurrection men" had got to them, exploiting the lucrative trade with the hospitals, where doctors cut up corpses for research purposes.

'Twas in the middle of the night,
　To sleep young William tried;
When Mary's ghost came stealing in,
　And stood at his bed-side.

O William dear! O William dear!
　My rest eternal ceases;
Alas! my everlasting peace
　Is broken into pieces.

I thought the last of all my cares
　Would end with my last minute;
But tho' I went to my long home,
　I didn't stay long in it.

The body-snatchers they have come
　And made a snatch at me;
It's very hard them kind of men
　Won't let a body be!

You thought that I was buried deep,
　Quite decent like and chary,
But from her grave in Mary-bone,
　They've come and boned your Mary.

The arm that used to take your arm
　Is took to Doctor Vyse;
And both my legs are gone to walk
　The hospital at Guy's.

I vowed that you should have my hand,
　But fate gives us denial;
You'll find it there, at Doctor Bell's,
　In spirits and a phial.

As for my feet, my little feet,
　You used to call so pretty,
There's one, I know, in Bedford Row,
　The t'other's in the City.

I can't tell where my head is gone,
　But Doctor Carpue can;
As for my trunk, it's all packed up
　To go by Pickford's van.

I wish you'd go to Mr. P.
　And save me such a ride;
I don't half like the outside place,
　They've took for my inside.

The cock it crows – I must be gone!
  My William, we must part!
But I'll be yours in death, altho'
  Sir Astley has my heart.

Don't go to weep upon my grave,
  And think that there I be;
They haven't left an atom there
  Of my anatomie.

"The Resurrection or an Internal View of the Museum in W—d—ll Street on The Last Day" by Thomas Rowlandson

AUGUSTIN DALY (1839–99)

Tied to the Railway Tracks
(from *Under The Gaslight*, 1867)

This extract is a joy to read for its wonderful, serious use of melodrama. The only unusual feature is that it's not the woman who is tied to the railway line – perhaps that had to wait for early Hollywood films. Without recounting the plot so far, it's enough to explain that the faithful old veteran Snorkey is tracking the evil Byke and his accomplices, while Laura has run away from the man who loves her. Now read on . . .

Act 4 Scene 3

Railroad Station at Shrewsbury Bend. Up Right the Station shed. Platform around it, and door at side, window in front. At Left clump of shrubs and tree. The Railroad track runs from across the back. View of Shrewsbury River in perspective. Night. Moonlight. The switch, with a red lantern and Signalman's coat hanging on it Left Centre. The Signal lamp and post beside it.

As the scene opens, several packages are lying about the Stage, among them a bundle of axes. The Signalman is wheeling in a small barrel from Left whistling at his work. Enter Laura in walking dress.

Laura   It is impossible for me to go further. A second time I've fled from home and friends, but now they will never find me. The trains must all have passed, and there are no conveyances till tomorrow. (*She sits at clump*)

Signalman   Beg pardon, ma'am, looking for anybody?

Laura   Thank you, no. Are you the man in charge of this station?

Signalman   Yes, ma'am.

Laura   When is there another train for New York?

Signalman   New York? Not till morning. We've only one more train tonight; that's the down one; it'll be here in about twenty minutes – "Express Train".

Laura   What place is that?

Signalman   That? That's the signal station shed. It serves for store-room, depot, baggage-room, and everything.

Laura   Can I stay there tonight?

Signalman   There? Well it's an odd place, and I should think you would hardly like it. Why don't you go to the hotel?

Laura   I have my reasons – urgent ones. It is not because I want money. You shall have this (*producing a purse*) if you let me remain here.

Signalman   Well. I've locked up a good many things in there over night, but I never had a young lady for freight before. Besides, ma'am, I don't know anything about you. You know it's odd that you won't go to a decent hotel, and plenty of money in your pocket.

Laura   You refuse me – well – I shall only have to sit here all night.

Signalman   Here, in the open air? Why, it would kill you.

Laura   So much the better.

Signalman   Excuse me for questions, Miss, but you're a running away from someone, ain't you?

Laura   Yes.

Signalman   Well, I'd like to help you. I'm a plain man you know and I'd like to help you, but there's one thing would go agin' me to assist in. (*Laura interested.*) I'm on to fifty years of age, and I've many children, some on 'em daughters grown. There's a many temptations for young gals, and sometimes the old man has to put on the brakes a bit, for some young men are wicked enough to persuade the gals to steal out of their father's house in the dead of night, and go to shame and misery. So tell me this – it ain't the old man, and the old man's home you've left, young lady?

Laura   No; you good, honest fellow – no – I have no father.

Signalman   Then, by Jerusalem! I'll do for you what I can. Anything but run away from them that have not their interest but yours at heart. Come, you may stay there, but I'll have to lock you in.

Laura   I desire that you should.

Signalman   It's for your safety as much as mine. I've got a patent lock on that door that would give a skeleton key the rheumatism to fool with it. You don't mind the baggage. I'll have to put it in with you, hoes, shovels, mowing machines, and what is this – axes. Yes, a bundle of axes. If the Superintendent finds me out, I'll ask him if he was afraid you'd run off with these. (*Laughs*) So, if you please, I'll first tumble 'em in. (*Puts goods in house, Laura sitting on platform looking at him. When all in, he comes towards her, taking up cheese-box to put it in Station*). I say, Miss, I ain't curious – but, of course, it's a young man you're a going to?

Laura   So far from that, it's a young man I'm running away from.

Signalman   (*dropping box*) Running away from a young man! Let me shake hands with you. (*Shakes her hand*) Lord, it does my heart good! At your age, too! (*Seriously*) I wish you'd come and live down in my neighbourhood a while, among my gals. (*Shaking his head*) You'd do a power of good. (*Putting box in station*)

Laura I've met an excellent friend. And here at least I can be concealed until tomorrow – then for New York. My heart feels lighter already – it's a good omen.

Signalman Now, Miss, bless your heart, here's your hotel ready.

Goes to switch and takes coat off, putting it on.

Laura Thanks, my good friend; but not a word to any one – till tomorrow; not even – not even to your girls.

Signalman Not a word, I promise you. If I told my girls, it would be over the whole village before morning.

She goes in. He locks door. Laura appears at window facing audience.

Laura Lock me in safely.

Signalman Ah! be sure I will. There! (*Tries door*) Safe as a jail. (*Pulls out watch, and then looking at track with lantern.*) Ten minutes and down she comes. It's all safe this way, my noisy beauty, and you may come as soon as you like. Good night, Miss!

Laura (*at window*) Good night.

Signalman Running away from a young man, Ha! ha! ha!

He goes to track, then looks down Right – lights his pipe and is trudging off Right, when enter Snorkey from Left.

Snorkey Ten minutes before the train comes. I'll wait here for it. (*To Signalman who re-enters*) Hollo, I say, the train won't stop here too long will it.

Signalman Too long? It won't stop here at all.

Snorkey I must reach the shore tonight. There'll be murder done, unless I can prevent it!

Signalman Murder, or no murder, the train can't be stopped.

Snorkey It's a lie. By waving the red signal for danger, the engineer must stop, I tell you!

Signalman Do you think I'm a fool! What! disobey orders and lose my place; then what's to become of my family? (*Exit*)

Snorkey I won't be foiled. I will confiscate some farmer's horse about here, and get there before them somehow. (*Byke enters at back with loose coil of rope in his hand.*) Then when Byke arrives in his donkey cart he'll be ready to sit for a picture of surprise.

Byke suddenly throws the coil over Snorkey.

Byke Will he?

Snorkey Byke!

Byke Yes, Byke. Where's that pistol of yours? (*Tightening rope round his arm.*)

Snorkey   In my breast pocket.

Byke   (*taking it*) Just what I wanted.

Snorkey   You ain't a going to shoot me?

Byke   No!

Snorkey   Well, I'm obliged to you for that.

Byke   (*leading him to platform*) Just sit down a minute, will you.

Snorkey   What for? (*Laura appears horror struck at window.*)

Byke   You'll see.

Snorkey   Well, I don't mind if I do take a seat. (*Sits down. Byke coils the rope round his legs.*) Hollo! what's this?

Byke   You'll see. (*Picks the helpless Snorkey up.*)

Snorkey   Byke, what are you going to do!

Byke   Put you to bed. (*Lays him across the track.*)

Snorkey   Byke, you don't mean to – My God, you are a villain!

Byke   (*fastening him to rails*) I'm going to put you to bed. You won't toss much. In less than ten minutes you'll be sound asleep. There, how do you like it? You'll get down to the Branch before me, will you? You dog me and play the eavesdropper, eh! Now do it if you can. When you hear the thunder under your head and see the lights dancing in your eyes, and feel the iron wheels a foot from your neck, remember Byke!
(*Exit*)

Laura   O, Heavens! he will be murdered before my eyes! How can I aid him?

Snorkey   Who's that?

Laura   It is I. Do you not know my voice?

Snorkey   That I do; but I almost thought I was dead, and it was an angel's. Where are you?

Laura   In the station.

Snorkey   I can't see you, but I can hear you. Listen to me, Miss, for I've got only a few minutes to live.

Laura   (*shaking door*) God help me or I cannot aid you.

Snorkey   Never mind me, Miss. I might as well die now, and here, as at any other time. I'm not afraid. I've seen death in almost every shape, and none of them scare me; but, for the sake of those you love, I would live. Do you hear me?

Laura   Yes! yes!

Snorkey   They are on the way to your cottage – Byke and Judas – to rob and murder.

Laura   (*in agony*) O I must get out! (*Shakes the window bars*) What shall I do?

Snorkey   Can't you burst the door?

Laura   It is locked fast.

Snorkey   Is there nothing in there? – no hammer? – no crowbar?

A poster advertising the play

Laura Nothing! (*Faint steam whistle heard in the distance.*) O, heavens! The train! (*Paralysed for an instant.*) The axe!!

Snorkey Cut the woodwork! Don't mind the lock – cut round it! How my neck tingles! (*A blow at door is heard.*) Courage! (*Another*) Courage! (*The steam whistle is heard again – nearer, and rumble of train on track. Another blow.*) That's a true woman! Courage! (*Noise of locomotive heard – with whistle. A last blow; the door swings open, mutilated – the lock hanging – and Laura appears, axe in hand.*) Here – quick! (*She runs and unfastens him. The locomotive lights glare on scene.*) Victory! Saved! Hooray! (*Laura leans exhausted against switch.*) And these are the women who ain't to have a vote!

As Laura takes his head from the track, the train of cars rushes past with roar and whistle from Left to Right.

GEORGE DIBDIN PITT (1799–1855)

Sweeney's Pork Pies
(from *The String of Pearls*, 1847)

The story of Sweeney Todd, the Demon Barber, is wonderfully gruesome and was so popular that it appeared in many stories and several other plays. The devilish Sweeney, the intriguing mechanism of the chair and the awful, stomach-turning recycling of the bodies through the pie shop are difficult to beat as a combination for macabre entertainment. This extract is the complete first act and, again, it takes on another life when it is performed.

Act 1 Scene 1

Interior of Sweeney Todd's Shop. A revolving trap, which has a similar chair beneath, so that whichever side is shown to the audience, the position of the chair and its appearance are the same.

Sweeney Todd discovered dressing a wig, and Tobias Ragg attending him.

Sweeney You will remember now, Tobias Ragg, that you are my apprentice; that you have had of me board, lodging, and washing, save that you take your meals at home, that you don't sleep here, and that your mother gets up your linen. (*fiercely*) Now, are you not a fortunate, happy dog?

Tobias (*timidly*) Yes, sir.

Sweeney You will acquire a first-rate profession, quite as good as the law, which your mother tells me that she would have put you to, only that a little weakness of the head-piece unqualified you. And now, Tobias, listen.

Tobias (*trembling*) Yes, sir.

Sweeney I'll cut your throat from ear to ear if you repeat one word of what passes in this shop, or are to make any supposition, or draw any conclusion from anything you may see or hear, or fancy you see or hear. Do you understand me?

Tobias   I won't say anything, Mr. Todd; if I do, may I be made into veal pies at Lovett's in Bell Yard.

Sweeney   (*starts*) How dare you mention veal pies in my presence? Do you suspect?

Tobias   Oh, sir; I don't suspect – indeed I don't! I meant no harm in making the remark.

Sweeney   (*eyes Tobias narrowly*) Very good. I'm satisfied – quite satisfied; and, mark me, the shop, and the shop only, is your place.

Tobias   Yes, sir.

Enter Mark Ingestrie, dressed as a sea-captain of the period.

Mark   By the description, this should be the man I seek. He can doubt-less give me some tidings of Johanna, and I can look forward to a happy meeting after an estrangement of many long and tedious years. Good morrow, friend; I have need of your craft. Let me get shaved at once, as I have to see a lady.

Sweeney   Happy to be of service to you, good gentleman. Will you be pleased to seat yourself? (*Brushes Mark's hair*) You've been to sea, sir?

Mark   Yes; and I have only now lately come up the river from an Indian voyage.

Sweeney   You carry some treasures, I presume?

Mark   Among others, this small casket. (*Mark produces it.*)

Sweeney   A piece of exquisite workmanship.

Mark   It is not the box but its contents that must cause you wonder, for I must, in confidence, tell you it contains a string of veritable pearls of the value of twelve thousand pounds.

Sweeney   (*chuckling aside, and whetting his razor on his hand*) I shall have to polish him off. Ha ha ha! heugh!

Mark   What the devil noise was that?

Sweeney   It was only me. I laughed. By the way, Tobias, while I am operating upon this gentleman's chin, the figures at St. Dunstan's are about to strike; the exhibition will excite your curiosity and allow me time to shave our customer without your interruption.

Tobias goes out.

Sweeney   Now sir, we can proceed to business, if it so please you; it's well you came here, sir, for though I say it, there isn't a shaving shop in the City of London that ever thinks upon polishing off a customer as I do – fact – can assure you – ha, ha! heugh!

Mark   Shiver the main-brace! I tell you what it is, Master Barber: if you come that laugh again, I will get up and go.

Sweeney   Very good, it won't occur again. (*Commences to mix up a lather*) If I am so bold, who are you? – where did you come from? – and whither are you going?

Mark   You seem fond of asking questions, my friend; perhaps before I answer them, you will reply to one I'm about to put?

Sweeney   Oh, yes, of course; what is it?

Mark   Do you know a Mr. Oakley, who lives somewhere hereabouts? He is a spectacle maker.

Sweeney   Yes, to be sure I do – Jasper Oakley, in Fore Street. Bless me, where can my strop be? I had it this minute – I must have lain it down somewhere. What an odd thing I can't see it. Oh, I recollect – I took it into the parlour. Sit still, sir, I shan't be a minute; you can amuse yourself with the newspaper. I shall soon polish him off!

Sweeney hands paper and goes out. A rushing noise heard, and Mark seated on the chair sinks through stage. After a pause, the chair rises vacant, and Sweeney enters. He examines the string of pearls which he holds in his hand.

Sweeney   When a boy, the thirst of avarice was first awakened by the fair gift of a farthing; that farthing soon became a pound; the pound a hundred – so to a thousand, till I said to myself, I will possess a hundred thousand. This string of pearls will complete the sum. (*Starts*) Who's there? (*Pounces upon Tobias, who has cautiously opened the door.*) Speak – and speak the truth, or your last hour has come! How long were you peeping through the door before you came in?

Tobias   Please, sir, I wasn't peeping at all.

Sweeney   Well, well, if you did peep, what then? It's no matter. I only wanted to know, that's all. It was quite a joke, wasn't it? Come now, there's no harm done, we'll be merry over it – very merry.

Tobias   (*puzzled*) Yes, very merry.

Sweeney   Who's that at the door?

Tobias   It's only the servant of the gentleman who came here to be shaved this morning.

Sweeney   Tell the fellow his master's not here; go – let him seek elsewhere, do you hear? I know I shall have to polish that boy off!

Whets his razor on his hand. As Sweeney concludes this speech, Tobias discovers the hat worn by Mark; this he secretes and goes out.

Enter Jean Parmine.

Jean   Good evening, neighbour; I would have you shave me.

Sweeney   Your servant, Mr. Parmine – you deal in precious stones.

Jean   Yes, I do; but it's rather late for a bargain. Do you want to buy or sell?

Sweeney   To sell.

Produces a casket and gives it to Jean.

Jean   (*examining pearls*) Real, by heaven, all real.

Sweeney   I know they are real. Will you deal with me or not?

Jean   I'm not quite sure that they are real; let me look at them again? Oh, I see, counterfeit; but so well done that really for the curiosity of the thing I will give you £50.

Sweeney   £50? Who is joking now, I wonder? We cannot deal tonight.

Jean   Stay – I will give you a hundred.

Sweeney   Hark ye, friend, I know the value of pearls.

Jean   Well, since you know more than I gave you credit for I think I can find a customer who will pay £11,000 for them; if so, I have no objection to advance the sum of £8,000.

Sweeney   I am content – let me have the money early tomorrow.

Jean   Stop a bit; there are some rather important things to consider – you must know that a string of pearls is not to be bought like a few ounces of old silver, and the vendor must give every satisfaction as to how he came by them.

Sweeney   (*aside*) I am afraid I shall have to polish him off. (*aloud*) In other words, you don't care how I possess the property, provided I sell it to you at a thief's price; but if, on the contrary, I want their real value, you mean to be particular.

Jean   I suspect you have no right to dispose of the pearls, and to satisfy myself I shall insist upon your accompanying me to a magistrate.

Sweeney   And what road shall you take?

Jean   The *right* path.

As Jean turns, Sweeney springs upon him. A fierce struggle ensues. Sweeney succeeds in forcing Jean into the chair. Sweeney touches a spring, and the chair sinks with a dreadful crash. Sweeney laughs and exclaims, "I've polished him off!" as scene closes.

Scene 2

Breakfast Parlour in the house of Jasper Oakley. Enter Johanna.

Johanna   Oh, Mark, Mark! why do you thus desert me when I have relied so abundantly on your true affection? Oh, why have you not sent me some token of your existence and of your continual love? The merest, slightest word would have been sufficient, and I should have been happy! Hark, what was that? I'm sure I heard footsteps beneath the chamber window.

Colonel Jeffery, enveloped in a cloak, enters.

Jeffery   I have the honour of speaking to Miss Johanna Oakley?

Johanna   Oh, sir, your looks are sad and serious! You seem about to announce some misfortune; tell me if it is not so.

Jeffery Let me pray you, lady, to subdue this passion of grief, and listen with patience to what I shall unfold. There is much to hear and much to speculate upon, and if from all that I have learnt, I cannot, dare not tell you Mark Ingestrie lives, I shrink likewise from telling you he is no more!

Johanna Speak again! – say those words again! – there is hope then – there is hope!

Jeffery You are aware that a quarrel with his uncle caused him to embark on an adventure in the Indian Seas?

Johanna Too well. Alas! it was on my account he sacrificed himself.

Jeffery Nay, good fortune attended that enterprise, and Mark Ingestrie showed me on our homeward voyage a string of pearls of immense value, which he said he intended for you. When we reached the River Thames, only three days since, he left the vessel for that purpose.

Johanna Alas! he never came.

Jeffery No; from all inquiries we can make, and from all information we can obtain, it seems that he disappeared somewhere in Fleet Street.

Johanna Disappeared!

Jeffery We can trace him to Temple Stairs, and from thence to a barber's shop kept by a man named Sweeney Todd; but beyond, we have no clue. It is necessary, Miss Oakley, that I now leave you, but you must promise to meet me –

Johanna When and where?

Jeffery At the hour of six this day week, in the Temple Gardens. I ask this of you because I am resolved to make all the exertion in my power to discover what has become of Mark Ingestrie, in whose fate I am sure I have succeeded in interesting you, although you care so little for the "string of pearls" he intended for you.

Johanna I suppose it is too much for human nature to expect two blessings at once. I had the fond warm heart that loved me, without the fortune that would have enabled us to live in comfort, and now, when that is, perchance, within my grasp, the heart which was by far the most costly possession, lies buried in a grave – its bright influences, its glorious aspirations quenched for ever.

Jeffery You will meet me, then, as I request, to hear if I have any news for you?

Johanna I have the will to do so, but Heaven knows only if I may have the power.

Jeffery What do you mean?

Johanna I cannot tell what a week's anxiety may do. I do not know but a sick bed may be my resting-place till I exchange it for a coffin. I feel now my strength fail me, and am scarcely able to totter to my chamber. Farewell, sir, I owe you my best thanks.

Jeffery   Remember, I bid you adieu, with the hope of meeting you again.

Jeffery by this time has reached the door of the apartment. He hears some one without, and conceals himself behind it as Dr. Lupin enters.

Johanna   Lupin here! (*aside*) How unfortunate!

Lupin   Yes, maiden. I am that chosen vessel whom the profane call "Mealy Mouth". I come hither at the bidding of thy respected mother to partake of a vain mixture which rejoiceth in the name of "tea". (*detains her*)

Johanna   You will allow me a free passage from the room, if you please, Dr. Lupin.

Lupin   Thy mother hath decided that I take thee unto my bosom, even as a wedded wife.

Johanna   Absurd! Have you been drinking?

Lupin   I never drink, save when the spirit waxeth faint. (*Takes a bottle from his pocket, and drinks.*) 'Tis an ungodly practice. (*Drinks again – offering Johanna bottle*) Let me offer you *spiritual* consolation – hum! ha!

Johanna   Bless me! you have the hiccups.

Lupin   Yes; I – I rather think I have a little. Isn't it a shame that one so pious should have the hiccups? Hum – ha! hum – ha! Damn the hiccups – that is, I mean damn all backsliders!

Johanna   The miserable hypocrite!

Lupin   The fire of love rageth – it consumeth my very vitals. Peradventure I may extinguish the flame by the moisture of those ruby lips – nay, I am resolved. (*Lupin seizes Johanna.*)

Johanna   Unhand me, ruffian, or repent it!

Jeffery rushes forward, and belabours Lupin with scabbard of his sword. Jeffery escapes through door, Johanna secures key.

Lupin   Help! verily I am assailed. Robbers! fire! help!

The household run in armed with brooms, mops, and Lupin exhibits a black eye. On perceiving this, Mrs. Oakley screams and faints.

Scene 3

Interior of Lovett's Pie-shop in Bell Yard, Temple Bar, front scene. Enter Mrs. Lovett and Jarvis Williams, dressed in rags.

Mrs. L   Go away, my good fellow; we never give anything to beggars.

Jarvis   Don't you, mum? I ain't no beggar, mum, but a young man who is on the look-out for a situation. I thought as how you might recommend me to some *light* employment where they puts the *heavy* work out.

Mrs. L   Recommend you! – recommend a ragged wretch like you! Besides, what employment can we have but pie-making? We have a man already who suits us very well, with the exception that he, as you would do if we were to exchange, has grown contemptuous in his calling.

Jarvis   Ay, that is the way of the world. There is always sufficient argument by the rich against the poor and destitute to keep 'em so; but argifying don't mend the matter. I'll look after another job. (*Going.*)

Mrs. L   (*aside*) If he be unknown he is the very man for our purpose. (*aloud*) Stay, you have solicited employment of me, and I don't see why I should not make a trial of you. Follow me.

Jarvis   Where to?

Mrs. L   To the bakehouse, where I will show you what you have to do. You must promise never to leave it on any pretence.

Jarvis   Never to leave it!

Mrs. L   Never, unless you leave it for good and for all. If upon those conditions you choose to accept the situation, you may; if not, you can depart and leave it alone.

Jarvis   As Shakespeare says, "My proverty, and not my will consents."
Mrs. Lovett raises a trap-door in front of shop, and points to the descent.

Mrs. L   By this passage, young man, we must descend to the furnace and ovens, where I will show you how to manufacture the pies, feed the fires, and make yourself generally useful.

Music – They descend trap, which closes as the scene opens.

Scene 4

The Bakehouse. A gloomy cellar of vast extent and sepulchral appearance. A fitful glare issues from the various low-arched entrances in which a huge oven is placed.

Enter Mrs. Lovett and Jarvis down the steps.

Jarvis   I suppose I'm to have someone to assist me in this situation. One pair of hands could never do the work in such a place.

Mrs. L   Are you not content?

Jarvis   Oh, yes, only you spoke of having a man.

Mrs. L   He has gone to his *friends* – he has gone to some of his very *oldest friends*, who will be glad to see him. But now I must leave you a time. As long as you are industrious, you will get on very well; but as soon as you begin to get idle and neglect my orders, you will receive a piece of information that may –

Jarvis   What is it? I am of an inquiring disposition – you may as well give it me now.

Mrs. L No; I seldom find there is occasion for it at first; but, after a time, when you get well fed you are pretty sure to want it. Everybody who relinquishes this situation goes to his old *friends, friends* that he has not seen for many years! I shall return anon.

Mrs. Lovett goes out.

Jarvis What a strange manner of talking that respectable middle-aged female has! There seems to be something very singular in all she utters! It's very strange! And what a singular looking place, too – nothing visible but darkness. I think it would be quite unbearable if it wasn't for the delicious odour of the pies. Talking of pies, I fancy I could eat one. (*Takes a pie off tray, and eats voraciously.*) Beautiful! delicious! lots of gravy! (*He suddenly discovers a long hair, views it mysteriously, and winds it round his finger.*) Somebody's been combing their hair. I don't think that pie's a nice un. (*Puts part of eaten pie back, and takes another.*) This is better! Done to a turn! Extremely savoury! (*Puts his hand in his mouth*) What's this? A bone? No; a button! I don't think I like pies now. How did that button come into that pie! Oh, la! I'm very poorly!

At this moment a part of the wall gives way, and Jean Parmine, with an iron bar, forces a passage through the aperture he has made.

Oh, la! here's one of the murdered ghosts come to ax for his body, and it's been made into pies. Oh, la! Please it wasn't me. I was only engaged today.

Jean Silence, my friend; you have nothing to fear! I see, like myself, you have been lured into this den!

Jarvis Since you are flesh and blood, and not a ghost, perhaps you can inform me why such wholesale butchery has been indulged in.

Jean The object of the wretches has solely been robbery, and their victims people of supposed wealth. They have in all cases been inveigled into the shop of an infamous monster, named Sweeney Todd, a barber, residing in Fleet Street; here, by an ingenious contrivance, the unfortunate sufferers were lowered to the cellars beneath the house, murdered, and conveyed to this retreat, where a glowing furnace destroyed every trace of the crime.

Jarvis Well, I never!

Jean We must strike out some plan for our mutual deliverance. We are in Bell Yard, and to my certain knowledge the houses right and left have cellars. Now, surely, with a weapon such as this bar, willing hearts and arms that have not quite lost their powers, we may make our way from this horrible abode. (*Noise*) Hark! some one is approaching. Follow me!

Music – Jean and Jarvis retire through aperture – Sweeney enters.

Sweeney   Gathering clouds warn the mountaineer of the approaching storm; let them now warn me to provide against danger. I have too many enemies to be safe. I will dispose of them one by one, till no evidence of my guilt remain. My first step must be to stop the babbling tongue of Tobias Ragg. Mrs. Lovett, too, grows scrupulous and dissatisfied; I've had my eye on her for some time, and fear she intends mischief. A little poison, skilfully administered, may remove any unpleasantness in that quarter. Hum! – ha – heugh! Who's there! (*Turns and discovers Mrs. Lovett standing at his elbow.*)

Mrs. L   Sweeney Todd!

Sweeney   (*calmly*) Well!

Mrs. L   Since I discover that you intend treachery, I shall on the instant demand my share of the booty – aye, an equal share of the fruits of our mutual bloodshed.

Sweeney   (*with the same air of indifference*) Well, so you shall, if you are only patient; I will balance accounts with you in a minute.

Sweeney takes a book from his pocket, and runs his finger down the account.

Sweeney   £12,000, to a fraction!

Mrs. L   That is just £6,000 for each person, there being two of us.

Sweeney   But, Mistress Lovett, I must first have you to know that, before I hand you a coin, you will have to pay me for your support, lodging, and clothes.

Mrs. L   Clothes? Why, I haven't had a new dress for these six months!

Sweeney   Besides, am I to have nothing for your education? (*Draws his finger significantly across his throat*) Yes, for some years you have been totally provided for by me; and, after deducting that and the expenses of erecting furnaces, purchasing flour for your delicious pies, etc., etc., I find it leaves a balance of 16s 4¾d* in my favour, and I don't intend you to budge an inch till it is paid.

Mrs. L   You want to rob me; but you shall find, to your sorrow, I will have my due. (*She secretly draws a knife – Sweeney starts back on beholding the weapon.*) Now, villain! who triumphs? Put your name to a deed consigning the whole of the wealth blood has purchased, or you perish where you stand!

Sweeney   Idiot! you should have known Sweeney Todd better, and learnt that he is a man to calculate his chances. Behold! (*Draws a pistol from his breast, fires, and kills Mrs. Lovett.*) Now let the furnace consume the body as it would wheaten straw, and destroy all evidence of my guilt in this, as it has in my manifold deeds of blood.

Sweeney opens the furnace door, a fierce glare lights the stage – he drags the body of Mrs. Lovett to the ovens as Act drop falls.

---

* 16s 4¾d = roughly 82p in new money

CHAINED AND TRAPPED

MARY PRINCE (c.1788–c.1835)

The Pain of Slavery
(from *The History of Mary Prince – A West Indian Slave*, 1831)

Mary Prince escaped from slavery and published a record of her life. For this book to exist is achievement in itself, given all the circumstances which would work against her ever being able to give voice to what she had suffered, let alone present them in written form. It is a good read, too. You can hear her voice and begin to sense, with her, the precise conditions of her slavery. This extract is taken from the early part of her story in the West Indies. She managed to escape when she was brought to England and was able to gain her freedom by going to court.

O H DEAR! I cannot bear to think of that day, – it is too much. – It recalls the great grief that filled my heart, and the woeful thoughts that passed to and fro through my mind, whilst listening to the pitiful words of my poor mother, weeping for the loss of her children. I wish I could find words to tell you all I then felt and suffered. The great God above alone knows the thoughts of the poor slave's heart, and the bitter pains which follow such separations as these. All that we love taken away from us – oh, it is sad, sad! and sore to be borne! – I got no sleep that night for thinking of the morrow; and dear Miss Betsey was scarcely less distressed. She could not bear to part with her old playmates and she cried sore and would not be pacified.

The black morning at length came; it came too soon for my poor mother and us. Whilst she was putting on us the new osnaburgs* in which we were to be sold, she said, in a sorrowful voice, (I shall never forget it!) "See, I am *shrouding* my poor children; what a task for a mother!" – She then called Miss Betsey to take leave of us. "I am going to carry my little chickens to market," (these were her very words) "take your last look of them; may be you will see them no more." . . . When I

* osnaburgs: clothes made of coarse linen

left my dear little brothers and the house in which I had been brought up, I thought my heart would burst.

Our mother, weeping as she went, called me away with the children Hannah and Dinah, and we took the road that led to Hamble Town, which we reached about four o'clock in the afternoon. We followed my mother to the market-place, where she placed us in a row against a large house, with our backs to the wall and our arms folded across our breasts. I, as the eldest, stood first, Hannah next to me, then Dinah; and our mother stood beside, crying over us. My heart throbbed with grief and terror so violently, that I pressed my hands quite tightly across my breast, but I could not keep it still, and it continued to leap as though it would burst out of my body. But who cared for that? Did one of the many bystanders, who were looking at us so carelessly, think of the pain that wrung the hearts of the negro woman and her young ones? No, no! They were not all bad, I dare say, but slavery hardens white people's hearts towards the blacks; and many of them were not slow to make their remarks upon us aloud, without regard to our grief – though their light words fell like cayenne on the fresh wounds of our hearts. Oh those white people have small hearts who can only feel for themselves.

At length the vendue master*, who was to offer us for sale like sheep or cattle, arrived, and asked my mother which was the eldest. She said nothing, but pointed to me. He took me by the hand, and led me out into the middle of the street, and, turning me slowly round, exposed me to the view of those who attended the vendue. I was soon surrounded by strange men, who examined and handled me in the same manner that a butcher would a calf or a lamb he was about to purchase, and who talked about my shape and size in like words – as if I could no more understand their meaning than the dumb beasts. I was then put up for sale. The bidding commenced at a few pounds, and gradually rose to fifty-seven, when I was knocked down to the highest bidder; and the people who stood by said that I had fetched a great sum for so young a slave.

I then saw my sisters led forth, and sold to different owners; so that we had not the sad satisfaction of being partners in bondage. When the sale was over, my mother hugged and kissed us, and mourned over us, begging of us to keep up a good heart, and do our duty to our new masters. It was a sad parting; one went one way, one another, and our poor mammy went home with nothing.

My new master was a Captain I—, who lived at Spanish Point. After parting with my mother and sisters, I followed him to his store, and he gave me into the charge of his son, a lad about my own age, Master Benjy, who took me to my new home. I did not know where I was going,

---

* vendue master: person in charge of the public sale or auction

or what my new master would do with me. My heart was quite broken with grief, and my thoughts went back continually to those from whom I had been so suddenly parted. "Oh, my mother! my mother!" I kept saying to myself, "Oh, my mammy and my sisters and my brothers, shall I never see you again!"

It was night when I reached my new home. The house was large, and built at the bottom of a very high hill; but I could not see much of it that night. I saw too much of it afterwards. The stones and the timber were the best things in it; they were not so hard as the hearts of the owners.

The person I took the most notice of that night was a French Black called Hetty, whom my master took in privateering from another vessel, and made his slave. She was the most active woman I ever saw, and she was tasked to her utmost. A few minutes after my arrival she came in from milking the cows, and put the sweet-potatoes on for supper. She then fetched home the sheep, and penned them in the fold; drove home the cattle, and staked them about the pond side; fed and rubbed down my master's horse, and gave the hog and the cow their suppers; prepared the beds, and undressed the children, and laid them to sleep. I liked to look at her and watch all her doings, for hers was the only friendly face I had as yet seen, and I felt glad that she was there. She gave me my supper of potatoes and milk, and a blanket to sleep upon, which she spread for me in the passage before the door of Mrs. I—'s chamber.

I got a sad fright, that night. I was just going to sleep, when I heard a noise in my mistress's room; and she presently called out to inquire if some work was finished that she had ordered Hetty to do. "No, Ma'am, not yet," was Hetty's answer from below. On hearing this, my master started up from his bed, and just as he was, in his shirt, ran down stairs with a long cow-skin in his hand. I heard immediately after, the cracking of the thong, and the house rang to the shrieks of poor Hetty, who kept crying out, "Oh, Massa! Massa! me dead. Massa! have mercy upon me – don't kill me outright." – This was a sad beginning for me. I sat up upon my blanket, trembling with terror, like a frightened hound, and thinking that my turn would come next. At length the house became still, and I forgot for a little while all my sorrows by falling fast asleep.

The next morning my mistress set about instructing me in my tasks. She taught me to do all sorts of household work; to wash and bake, pick cotton and wool, and wash floors, and cook. And she taught me (how can I ever forget it!) more things than these; she caused me to know the exact difference between the smart of the rope, the cart-whip, and the cow-skin, when applied to my naked body by her own cruel hand. And there was scarcely any punishment more dreadful than the blows I received on my face and head from her hard heavy fist. She was a fearful woman, and a savage mistress to her slaves.

APHRA BEHN (1640–89)

Trusting the White Man
(from *Oroonoko*, 1688)

Aphra Behn's life reads like a novel. Her father died en route with the family to Surinam (the setting of part of this story). She married a wealthy Dutch merchant but he died, possibly of the plague, a year later. Aphra worked as a secret agent in Holland, found herself penniless and spent time in prison. She turned to writing and made enough money to live well, despite criticism: she wrote, "If I must not, because of my sex, have this freedom, I lay down my quill . . . I value fame as much as if I had been a hero; and if you rob me of that I can retire from the ungrateful world and scorn its fickle favours." Her plays, particularly **The Rover***, are better known. In this extract, the African prince, Oroonoko, has been invited with his friends to dine aboard an English ship.*

THE PRINCE having drank hard of Punch, and several Sorts of Wine, as did all the rest, (for great Care was taken they should want nothing of that Part of the Entertainment) was very merry, and in great Admiration of the Ship, for he had never been in one before; so that he was curious of beholding every Place where he decently might descend. The rest, no less curious, who were not quite overcome with drinking, rambled at their Pleasure *Fore* and *Aft*, as their Fancies guided 'em: So that the Captain, who had well laid his Design before, gave the Word, and seiz'd on all his Guests; they clapping great Irons suddenly on the Prince, when he was leap'd down into the Hold, to view that Part of the Vessel; and locking him fast down, secur'd him. The same Treachery was used to all the rest; and all in one Instant, in several Places of the Ship, were lash'd fast in Irons, and betray'd to Slavery. That great Design over, they set all Hands at Work to hoist Sail; and with as treacherous as fair a Wind they made from the Shore with this innocent and glorious Prize, who thought of nothing less than such an Entertainment.

Some have commended this Act, as brave in the Captain; but I will spare my Sense of it, and leave it to my Reader to judge as he pleases. It may be easily guess'd, in what Manner the Prince resented this Indignity, who may be best resembled to a Lion taken in a Toil; so he raged, so he struggled for Liberty, but all in vain: And they had so wisely managed his Fetters, that he could not use a Hand in his Defence, to quit himself of a Life that would by no Means endure Slavery; nor could he move from the Place where he was ty'd, to any solid Part of the Ship, against which he might have beat his Head, and have finish'd his Disgrace that Way. So that being deprived of all other Means, he resolv'd to perish for want of Food; and pleas'd at last with that Thought, and toil'd and tir'd by Rage and Indignation, he laid himself down, and sullenly resolv'd upon dying, and refused all Things that were brought him.

This did not a little vex the Captain, and the more so, because he found almost all of 'em of the same Humour; so that the Loss of so many brave Slaves, so tall and goodly to behold, would have been very considerable: He therefore order'd one to go from him (for he would not be seen himself) to *Oroonoko*, and to assure him, he was afflicted for having rashly done so unhospitable a Deed, and which could not be now remedied, since they were far from Shore; but since he resented it in so high a Nature, he assur'd him he would revoke his Resolution, and set both him and his Friends ashore on the next Land they should touch at; and of this the Messenger gave him his Oath, provided he would resolve to live. And *Oroonoko*, whose Honour was such, as he never had violated a Word in his Life himself, much less a solemn Asseveration, believ'd in an Instant what this Man said; but reply'd, He expected, for a Confirmation of this, to have his shameful Fetters dismis'd. This Demand was carried to the Captain; who return'd him Answer, That the Offence had been so great which he had put upon the Prince, that he durst not trust him with Liberty while he remain'd in the Ship, for fear, lest by Valour natural to him, and a Revenge that would animate that Valour, he might commit some Outrage fatal to himself, and the King his Master, to whom the Vessel did belong. To this *Oroonoko* reply'd, He would engage his Honour to behave himself in all friendly Order and Manner, and obey the Command of the Captain, as he was Lord of the King's Vessel, and General of those Men under his Command.

This was deliver'd to the still doubting Captain, who could not resolve to trust a Heathen, he said, upon his Parole, a Man that had no Sense or Notion of the God that he worshipp'd. *Oroonoko* then reply'd, He was very sorry to hear that the Captain pretended to the Knowledge and Worship of any Gods, who had taught him no better Principles, than not to credit as he would be credited. But they told him, the Difference of their Faith occasion'd that Distrust: for the Captain had protested to him upon the Word of a Christian, and sworn in the Name of a great God; which if he should violate, he must expect eternal Torments in the

World to come. "Is that all the Obligations he has to be just to his Oath? (reply'd *Oroonoko*) Let him know, I swear by my Honour; which to violate, would not only render me contemptible and despised by all brave and honest Men, and so give my self perpetual Pain, but it would be eternally offending and displeasing all Mankind; harming, betraying, circumventing, and outraging all Men. But Punishments hereafter are suffer'd by one's self; and the World takes no Cognizance whether this God has reveng'd 'em or not, 'tis done so secretly, and deferr'd so long; while the Man of no Honour suffers every Moment the Scorn and Contempt of the honester World, and dies every Day ignominiously in his Fame, which is more valuable than Life. I speak not this to move Belief, but to shew you how you mistake, when you imagine, that he who will violate his Honour, will keep his Word with his *Gods*." So, turning from him with a disdainful Smile, he refused to answer him, when he urged him to know what Answer he should carry back to his Captain; so that he departed without saying any more.

The Captain pondering and consulting what to do, it was concluded, that nothing but *Oroonoko's* Liberty would encourage any of the rest to eat, except the *Frenchman*, whom the Captain could not pretend to keep Prisoner, but only told him, he was secur'd, because he might act something in Favour of the Prince; but that he should be freed as soon as they came to Land. So that they concluded it wholly necessary to free the Prince from his Irons, that he might shew himself to the rest; that they might have an Eye upon him, and that they could not fear a single Man.

This being resolved, to make the Obligation the greater, the Captain himself went to *Oroonoko*; where, after many Compliments, and Assurances of what he had already promis'd, he receiving from the Prince his Parole, and his Hand, for his good Behaviour, dismiss'd his Irons, and brought him to his own Cabin; where, after having treated and repos'd him a While, (for he had neither eat nor slept in four Days before) he besought him to visit those obstinate People in Chains, who refused all manner of Sustenance; and intreated him to oblige 'em to eat, and assure 'em of their Liberty the first Opportunity . . .

After this, they no longer refus'd to eat, but took what was brought 'em, and were pleas'd with their Captivity, since by it they hoped to redeem the Prince, who, all the rest of the Voyage, was treated with all the Respect due to his Birth . . . he endur'd a tedious Voyage, and at last arriv'd at the Mouth of the River of *Surinam*, a Colony belonging to the King of *England*, and where they were to deliver some Part of their Slaves. There the Merchants and Gentlemen of the Country going on Board, to demand those Lots of Slaves they had already agreed on; and, amongst those, the Overseers of those Plantations where I then chanc'd to be: The Captain, who had given the Word, order'd his Men to bring up those noble Slaves in Fetters, whom I have spoken of; and having put 'em, some in one, and some in other Lots, with Women and Children, (which they call *Pickaninies*) they sold 'em off, as Slaves to several Merchants and Gentlemen; not putting any two in one Lot, because they would separate 'em far from each other; nor daring to trust 'em together, lest Rage and Courage should put 'em upon contriving some great Action, to the Ruin of the Colony.

Oroonoko was first seiz'd on, and sold to our Overseer, who had the first Lot, with seventeen more of all Sorts and Sizes, but not one of Quality with him. When he saw this, he found what they meant; for, as I said, he understood *English* pretty well; and being wholly unarm'd and defence-less, so as it was in vain to make any Resistance, he only beheld the Captain with a Look all fierce and disdainful, upbraiding him with Eyes that forc'd Blushes on his guilty Cheeks, he only cry'd in passing over the Side of the Ship; *Farewell, Sir, 'tis worth my Sufferings to gain so true a Knowledge, both of you, and of your Gods, by whom you swear.* And desiring those that held him to forbear their Pains, and telling 'em he would make no Resistance, he cry'd, *Come, my Fellow-Slaves, let us descend, and see if we can meet with more Honour and Honesty in the next World we shall touch upon.* So he nimbly leapt into the Boat, and shewing no more Concern, suffer'd himself to be row'd up the River, with his seventeen Companions.

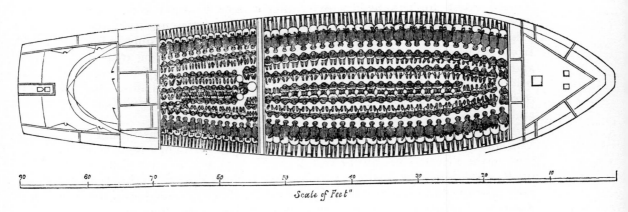

Scale of Feet"

Ship plans showing how the slaves were packed in.

PO CHÜ-I (772–840)

Losing a Slave Girl (c.829)
(translated by Arthur Waley)

This is a poem which shines out from the darkness of time through that wonderfully precise way that the Chinese catch thought and the human voice. It's startling because it comes from such a long time back and offers a point of a view which is totally unexpected.

AROUND MY GARDEN the little wall is low;
In the bailiff's lodge the lists are seldom checked.
I am ashamed to think we were not always kind;
I regret your labours, that will never be repaid.
The caged bird owes no allegiance;
The wind-tossed flower does not cling to the tree.

Where tonight she lies none can give us news
Nor any knows, save the bright watching moon.

The Slavery of Poverty – two letters

The first of these letters (c. 1885) was quoted by William (General) Booth of the Salvation Army to illustrate the horrors of the poverty he saw around him. Many of the conditions that he laments, including seeing people forced to bed down for the night in doorways, hardly seem distant. This letter, by a chemist to his brother, was read out at the chemist's trial after he had poisoned his only child and tried, with his wife, to commit suicide.

MY DEAREST GEORGE – Twelve months have I now passed of a most miserable and struggling existence, and I really cannot stand it any more. I am completely worn out, and relations who could assist me won't do any more, for such was uncle's last intimation. Never mind; he can't take his money and comfort with him, and in all probability will find himself in the same boat as myself. He never enquires whether I am starving or not. £3 – a mere flea-bite to him – would have put us straight, and with his security and good interest might have obtained me a good situation long ago. I can face poverty and degradation no longer, and would sooner die than go to the workhouse, whatever may be the awful consequences of the steps we have taken. We have, God forgive us, taken our darling Arty with us out of pure love and affection, so that the darling should never be cuffed about, or reminded or taunted with his heartbroken parents' crime. My poor wife has done her best at needle-work, washing, house-minding, etc., in fact, anything and everything that would bring in a shilling; but it would only keep us in semi-starvation. I have now done six weeks' travelling from morning till night, and not received one farthing for it. If that is not enough to drive you mad – wickedly mad – I don't know what is. No bright prospect anywhere; no ray of hope.

May God Almighty forgive us for this heinous sin, and have mercy on our sinful souls, is the prayer of your miserable, broken-hearted, but loving brother, Arthur. We have now done everything that we can possibly think of to avert this wicked proceeding, but can discover no ray of hope. Fervent prayer has availed us nothing; our lot is cast, and we must abide by it. It must be God's will or He would have ordained it differently. Dearest Georgy, I am exceedingly sorry to leave you all, but I am mad – thoroughly mad. You, dear, must try and forget us, and, if possible, forgive us; for do not consider it our own fault we have not succeeded. If you could get £3 for our bed it will pay our rent, and our scanty furniture may fetch enough to bury us in a cheap way. Don't grieve over us or follow us, for we shall not be worthy of such respect. Our clergyman has never called on us or given us the least consolation, though I called on him a month ago. He is paid to preach, and there he considers his responsibility ends, the rich excepted. We have only yourself and a very few others who care one pin what becomes of us, but you must try and forgive us, is the last fervent prayer of your devotedly fond and affectionate but broken-hearted and persecuted brother.

(Signed) R.A.O—.

This second letter was sent to James Bailey, a Justice of the Peace, and then printed in a newspaper. It is just one attempt of many to voice the deep anger and frustration about enforced poverty. "Shul de hill" in Manchester, at the end of the letter, is a reference to the fight there, a few years earlier, when several people had been killed.

Rosandale August 21 1762.

THIS HIS to asquaint you that We poor of Rosendale Rochdale Oldham Saddleworth Ashton have all mutaly and firmly agreed by Word and Covinent and Oath to Fight and Stand by Each Other as long as Life doth last for We may as well all be hanged as starved to Death and to see ower Children weep for Bread and none to give Them nor no liklyness of ever mending wile You all take Part with Brommal and Markits drops at all the princable Markits elceware but take This for a shure Maxon, That if You dont put those good Laws in Execution against all Those Canables or Men Slayers That have the Curse of God and all honest Men both by Gods Laws and Mens Laws so take Notice Bradshaw Bailey and Lloyd the biggest Rogue of all Three I know You all have Power to stop such vilonas Proceedings if You please and if You dont amaidatley put a Stopp and let hus feel it the next Saturday We will murder You all that We have down in Ower List and Wee will all bring a Faggot and burn down Your Houses and Wait Houses and make Your Wifes Widdows and Your Children Fatherless for the Blood of Shul de hill lyes cloose at Ower Harts and Blood for Blood We Require.

Take Care. Middleton.

Children at Work

The Climbing Boys – "As bad as the negro slavery"

*Climbing boys (and girls) were apprenticed to chimney sweeps and sent up chimneys which were particularly difficult to clean. In contrast to the sentimental view presented by Charles Kingsley in **The Water Babies,** the evidence to Parliamentary investigators describes the awful details of the job.*

London, Dec. 31

The dangerous practice of forcing little chimney sweeps to climb up a nich on the outside of St. George's Church, Hanover Square, still continues. A dirty brute, was yesterday employed for near two hours in forcing a child, at the risk of his life, to climb up the place alluded to; sometimes by sending another lad to poke him up, by putting his head underneath him, and at others by pricking him with a pin fastened to the end of a stick. The poor child, in the struggles to keep himself from falling, had rubbed the skin from his knees and elbows, while the perspiration arising from fear and exertion covered his face and breast as if water had been thrown upon him.

(from) The Lady's Magazine, or Entertaining Companion for the Fair Sex, 1802

ON MONDAY MORNING, March 29 1813, a chimney-sweeper of the name of Griggs attended to sweep a small chimney in the brewhouse of Messrs Calvert and Co. in Upper Thames Street; he was accompanied by one of his boys, a lad of about eight years of age, of the name of Thomas Pitt. The fire had been lighted as early as 2 o'clock the same morning, and was burning on the arrival of Griggs and his little boy at eight. The fireplace was small, and an iron pipe projected from the grate some little way into the flue. This the master was acquainted with (having swept the chimneys in the brewhouse for some years), and therefore had a tile or two broken from the roof, in order that the boy might descend the chimney. He had no sooner extinguished the fire than he suffered the lad to go down; and the consequence, as might be expected, was his almost immediate death, in a state, no doubt, of inexpressible agony. The flue was of the narrowest description, and must have retained heat sufficient to have prevented the child's return to the top, even supposing he had not approached the pipe belonging to the grate, which must have been nearly red hot; this however was not clearly ascertained on the inquest, though the appearance of the body would induce an opinion that he had been unavoidably pressed against the pipe. Soon after his descent, the master, who remained on the top, was apprehensive that something had happened, and therefore desired him to come up; the answer of the boy was, "I cannot come up, master, I must die here." An alarm was given in the brewhouse immediately that he had stuck in the chimney, and a bricklayer who was at work near the spot attended, and after knocking down part of the brickwork of the chimney, just above the fireplace, made a hole sufficiently large to draw him through. A surgeon attended, but all attempts to restore life were ineffectual. On inspecting the body, various burns appeared; the fleshy part of the legs and a great part of the feet more particularly were injured; those parts too by which climbing boys most effectually ascend or descend chimneys, viz. the elbows and knees, seemed burnt to the bone; from which it must be evident that the unhappy sufferer made some attempts to return as soon as the horrors of his situation became apparent.

(from) Minutes of evidence taken before the Parliamentary Committee on Employment of boys in sweeping chimneys, June 23 1817

Mr. George Ruff, of Upper Parliament Street, Nottingham, in evidence. I am a chimney-sweeper, and also own a shop here . . . The use of boys is much encouraged by the fact that many householders will have their chimneys swept by boys instead of by machinery. I have myself lost a great amount of custom which I should otherwise have . . . I have been sent away even from magistrates' houses, and in some cases even by ladies who have professed to pity the boys, for refusing to use them.

However, to satisfy particular customers, and in order to be able to do jobs where perhaps one chimney out of a lot would need a boy, I did for a time try to bring up one of my own children to it, but my wife and I felt that we could not stand it any longer, and that we would sooner go to the workhouse than suffer what we did from it.

No one knows the cruelty which a boy has to undergo in learning. The flesh must be hardened. This is done by rubbing it, chiefly on the elbows and knees with the strongest brine, as that got from a pork-shop, close by a hot fire. You must stand over them with a cane, or coax them by a promise of a halfpenny, etc. if they will stand a few more rubs.

At first they will come back from their work with their arms and knees streaming with blood, and the knees looking as if the caps had been pulled off. Then they must be rubbed with brine again, and perhaps go off at once to another chimney. In some boys I have found that the skin does not harden for years.

The best age for teaching boys is about six. That is thought a nice trainable age. But I have known two at least of my neighbours' children begin at the age of five. I once saw a child only $4\frac{1}{2}$ years in the market place in his sooty clothes and with his scraper in his hand. Some said, "Look at that little fellow, he is not 4". But one man standing by said, "He's $4\frac{1}{2}$; his father (naming him) told me his birthday, and said that he began when he was 4, and that he would make a nice little climber."

Nottingham is famous for climbing boys. This is on account of the chimneys being so narrow. A Nottingham boy is . . . worth more to sell.

A boy of about 7 or 8 was stolen from me once. As he was in the street a man seized him in his arms, carried him off to a lodging-house, and stupefied him with drugged tea. After the tea the child fell into deep sleep and lost all his appetite. An inspector and I traced him to Hull. The boy was so glad to find that "master" had come. The man had said that if they had got him to France, they should have had £10 for him. The stealer was a sweep of Hull; letters were found on him giving orders for more boys, and these letters were read before the magistrate. The prosecution was afterwards dropped, as the magistrates said that the man must be transported for kidnapping, if it was pressed. However, he said he would not do it again, and paid more than £20 for the expenses. I would not keep any boys after that. . .

Seven or eight years ago a boy was smothered in a chimney here. The doctor (naming him) who opened his body, said that they had pulled his heart and liver all out of place in dragging him down. . .

Formerly the sweeps, as they said themselves, had three washes a year, viz. at Whitsuntide, Goose Fair (October), and Christmas. But now they are quite different. This is owing a great deal I think to a rule which we brought about of taking no orders after twelve midday, and washing then. The object of this was to let boys go to school in the afternoon.

At first most did, but they do not now. A lady complained to me because she could not get her chimney done, and said, "A chimney sweep, indeed, wanting education! what next?"

The day's work here generally begins at about 4 or 4½ a.m., and lasts for 12 hours, including going round for orders. A man and boy together will earn in a fair full day 6s., but perhaps one day they may sweep 20 chimneys, another half-a-dozen.

The younger boys are more valuable, as they can go up any chimney. When they get too big to climb, which in town chimneys is about 15, or 16, in the large country chimneys a few years older, they are unfitted for other employments and often do nothing. Many active young men sweeps have gone into the workhouse here after the spring cleaning is up, to spend the summer in idleness and come out again for the winter work.

THOMAS CLARKE, Goose Gate, Nottingham, in evidence: I have been a chimney-sweeper in Nottingham for 38 years; I am also a member of the Sweeps' Association here to prevent the employment of climbing boys. – The usual age at which boys begin now is from 6 upwards. I began myself at a little over 5. They are generally the children of the poorest and worse-behaved parents, who want to get rid of them and make a little money by it as well. It is as bad as the Negro slavery, only it is not so known. . .

I had myself formerly boys as young as 5½ years, but I did not like them; they were too weak. I was afraid they might go off. It is no light thing having a life lost in your service. They go off just as quietly as you might fall asleep in the chair, by the fire there. It is just as if you had two or three glasses of strong drink . . .

I have known eight or nine sweeps lose their lives by the sooty cancer. The parts (private) which it seizes, are entirely eaten off. There is no cure for it once it has begun. These diseases are caused entirely by "sleeping black", and breathing the soot in all night. I have seen a piece as big as a bean on the front teeth in the morning. What they breathe when at work they spit out. . .

The use of boys for climbing seems to harden the women more than the men. Only lately a woman who had put her child to a sweep followed me and threatened to pull my hair for speaking against having climbing boys.

Machines will do the work well, and are not dear. A common one with iron fittings may be had for 25s, a good one with brass fittings, which are much lighter, for less than £2, and the best of all with all extras complete, for £3. With yearly repairs and all I have not laid out more than equal to two new machines in 20 years, and parts of my first are still in use. There may be chimneys which cannot be swept by a machine, but I have never seen one . . .

(from) Evidence to Children's Employment Commission, 1863

A Good Worker

"My mother always brought me up to be a good worker"

This is remarkable for the way that the reporter attempts to convey the incredible work involved in carrying some 36 tons of bricks each day and the apparent contentment of twelve-year-old Ann. Punishing hours and work can't seem to dim her sense of duty, although she does look forward to a time when she might be "an angel . . . and sit in Jesus' lap".

MESSRS BAKER & CO.'s firebrick works, Brierly Hill: some girls and women were engaged in "drawing a kiln", i.e. taking out the baked bricks. A kiln is sometimes too hot to be entered at all, and the people are obliged to wait. This was warm at the doorway, and like an oven inside, where some stood, the others forming a line to hand or rather toss on the bricks, two at a time, from one to the other, to a cart outside, where they were being packed.

A small girl of twelve, forming one of the line, struck me by the earnest way in which she was doing her share of a work which certainly is heavy for a child, as a slight calculation shows. The kiln, containing 17,000 bricks, of 7¼lbs* each when dry, was to be emptied by ten persons in a day and a half; i.e. this girl had to catch and toss on to her neighbour in a day of only the usual length a weight of more than 36 tons, and in so doing to make backwards and forwards 11,333 complete half turns of her body, while raised from the ground on a sloping plank. The plank is said not to be needed all the time. When called down by me she was panting.

This, however, was not her regular work; but the work which had been exacted from her at another place when 10 years old is astonishing, involving often 15 or 16 hours of heavy work daily for long periods continuously, with very scanty and few meal-times. Her energy of manner and evident love of work, and her utter absence of all tone of complaint, were remarkable; but the contrast between her hard bodily work and the pictures called up in her mind by the mention of "angel" (see the girl's own story below) was still more striking. She was small, but healthy looking, and though ignorant very intelligent.

* 7¼lbs: 3.28 kg

ANN ELIZABETH POWELL, age 12 – Carrying bricks is my regular work, but today I am "drawing" a kiln. Get 6d* a day. Have an hour for dinner, and eat it here. Am only just come.

Went to a red-brick yard near, at 10 years old. No girls worked there but me and their own daughter. From 6 to 6 was the regular time, but they used to make me go there by 5 a.m. and stay till 8 p.m. for a fortnight, sometimes for a month together. It used to be as the missis told us. Have worked there till 8 every night, going in the morning as early as 6, for four months together. Did not stop for tea when we worked till 8. Had a quarter of an hour for breakfast and half an hour for dinner; did not work in that time. My work was carrying bricks and heaving clay. I carried enough clay for four bricks on my head, and for two in my arms. My head used to ache, but not my back. Got 4d a day, and the same when we stayed till 8. If we had worked till 12 it would have been just the same, but I never did so late as that, though I have often worked till 9 and $9\frac{1}{2}$ on the light nights in summer. Have done so for two weeks together, going at 6 in the morning. Never got beaten, and never got tired, not when staying late. I hope I shall never get tired of work. My mother always brought me up to be a good worker.

Was at a day school a little bit. Don't know all the letters. Don't know what an "ox" is. (*Asked of* "ship".) Yes; about our place they keep a many of them. ("Ship" *explained not to be* "sheep".) No; don't know what it is, or what the sea is. Father reads the Bible out, but he only comes home once t'a week. An angel is very pretty. I wished I was an angel. They live in heaven. I hope I shall be one some day, and sit in Jesus' lap. To be one I must behave very well.

(from) Mr. White's Report on the Metal Manufacturers of the Birmingham District, 1864.

* 6d: 2½p

ANON

Dahn the Plug'ole

Songs, sentimental and sensational, were an important part of Victorian life at all levels, best known through the Music Halls. This well-known song is a treat to perform. What is the tone – sad, funny, grotesque – and how should it be sung – plaintively, loud or accompanied by tragic gesture?

A MUVVER was barfin' 'er biby one night,
The youngest of ten and a tiny young mite,
The muvver was pore and the biby was thin,
Only a skelington covered in skin;
The muvver turned rahnd for the soap orf the rack,
She was but a moment, but when she turned back,
The biby was gorn; and in anguish she cried,
"Oh, where is my biby?" – the Angels replied:
"Your biby 'as fell dahn the plug'ole,
Your biby 'as gorn dahn the plug;
The poor little thing was so skinny and thin
'E oughter been barfed in a jug;
Your biby is perfectly 'appy,
'E won't need a barf any more,
Your biby 'as fell dahn the plug'ole,
Not lorst, but gorn before!"

MARY SHELLEY (1797–1851)

Frankenstein's Creation asks for Companionship
(from *Frankenstein*, 1818)

Mary Shelley was 18 when she wrote this astonishing book. The storytelling evening out of which it arose also provoked, from the poet Byron, an early version of a Dracula story. **Frankenstein** *is widely known but not widely read. The versions we have from films have taken the horror elements but not the human ones. Dr. Frankenstein creates a man who is often referred to as a "monster". The novel takes no simple view as to who is the more sympathetic or the more monstrous – the creation or Frankenstein who has attempted to play God and then abandoned the man he made. Here, Frankenstein's creation tries to explain to his maker the suffering that he has endured – "misery made me fiend". He has been abandoned, he is ugly but human.*

"It is with considerable difficulty that I remember the original era of my being; all the events of that period appear confused and indistinct. A strange multiplicity of sensations seized me, and I saw, felt, heard, and smelt at the same time; and it was, indeed, a long time before I learned to distinguish between the operations of my various senses. By degrees, I remember, a stronger light pressed upon my nerves, so that I was obliged to shut my eyes. Darkness then came over me and troubled me, but hardly had I felt this when, by opening my eyes, as I now suppose, the light poured in upon me again. I walked and, I believe, descended, but I presently found a great alteration in my sensations. Before, dark and opaque bodies had surrounded me, impervious to my touch or sight; but I now found that I could wander on at liberty, with no obstacles which I could not either surmount or avoid. The light became more and more oppressive to me, and the heat wearying me as I walked, I sought a place where I could receive shade. This was the forest near Ingolstadt; and here I lay by the side of a brook resting from my fatigue, until I felt tormented by hunger and thirst. This roused me from

my nearly dormant state, and I ate some berries which I found hanging on the trees or lying on the ground. I slaked my thirst at the brook, and then lying down, was overcome by sleep.

"It was dark when I awoke; I felt cold also, and half frightened, as it were, instinctively, finding myself so desolate. Before I had quitted your apartment, on a sensation of cold, I had covered myself with some clothes, but these were insufficient to secure me from the dews of night. I was a poor, helpless, miserable wretch; I knew, and could distinguish, nothing; but feeling pain invade me on all sides, I sat down and wept . . . And what was I? Of my creation and creator I was absolutely ignorant, but I knew that I possessed no money, no friends, no kind of property. I was, besides, endued with a figure hideously deformed and loathsome; I was not even of the same nature as man. I was more agile than they and could subsist upon coarser diet; I bore the extremes of heat and cold with less injury to my frame; my stature far exceeded theirs. When I looked around I saw and heard of none like me. Was I, then, a monster, a blot upon the earth, from which all men fled and whom all men disowned?

"I cannot describe to you the agony that these reflections inflicted upon me; I tried to dispel them, but sorrow only increased with knowledge. Oh, that I had forever remained in my native wood, nor known nor felt beyond the sensations of hunger, thirst, and heat!

"Of what a strange nature is knowledge! It clings to the mind, when it has once seized on it, like a lichen on the rock. I wished sometimes to shake off all thought and feeling, but I learnt that there was but one means to overcome the sensation of pain, and that was death – a state which I feared yet did not understand. I admired virtue and good feelings and loved the gentle manners and amiable qualities of my cottagers, but I was shut out from intercourse with them, except through means which I obtained by stealth, when I was unseen and unknown, and which rather increased than satisfied the desire I had of becoming one among my fellows. . . Miserable, unhappy wretch!

"Other lessons were impressed upon me even more deeply. I heard of the difference of sexes, and the birth and growth of children; how the father doated on the smiles of the infant, and the lively sallies of the older child; how all the life and cares of the mother were wrapped up in the precious charge; how the mind of youth expanded and gained knowledge; of brother, sister, and all the various relationships which bind one human being to another in mutual bonds.

"But where were my friends and relations? No father had watched my infant days, no mother had blessed me with smiles and caresses; or if they had, all my past life was now a blot, a blind vacancy in which I distinguished nothing. From my earliest remembrance I had been as I

then was in height and proportion. I had never yet seen a being resembling me or who claimed any intercourse with me. What was I? The question again recurred, to be answered only with groans. Like Adam, I was apparently united by no link to any other being in existence; but his state was far different from mine in every other respect. He had come forth from the hands of God a perfect creature, happy and prosperous, guarded by the especial care of his Creator; he was allowed to converse with and acquire knowledge from beings of a superior nature, but I was wretched, helpless, and alone. Many times I considered Satan as the fitter emblem of my condition, for often, like him, when I viewed the bliss of my protectors, the bitter gall of envy rose within me. . . 'Hateful day when I received life!' I exclaimed in agony. 'Accursed creator! Why did you form a monster so hideous that even *you* turned from me in disgust? God, in pity, made man beautiful and alluring, after his own image; but my form is a filthy type of yours, more horrid even from the very resemblance. Satan had had his companions, fellow devils, to admire and encourage him, but I am solitary and abhorred.'

"These were the reflections of my hours of despondency and solitude . . . Increase of knowledge only discovered to me more clearly what a wretched outcast I was. I cherished hope, it is true, but it vanished when I beheld my person reflected in water or my shadow in the moonshine, even as that frail image and that inconstant shade.

"I endeavoured to crush these fears . . . and sometimes I allowed my thoughts, unchecked by reason, to ramble in the fields of Paradise, and dared to fancy amiable and lovely creatures sympathising with my feelings and cheering my gloom; their angelic countenances breathed smiles of consolation. But it was all a dream; no Eve soothed my sorrows nor shared my thoughts; I was alone. I remembered Adam's supplication to his Creator. But where was mine? He had abandoned me, and in the bitterness of my heart I cursed him.

"Autumn passed thus. I saw, with surprise and grief, the leaves decay and fall, and nature again assume the barren and bleak appearance it had worn when I first beheld the woods and the lovely moon. Yet I did not heed the bleakness of the weather; I was better fitted by my conformation for the endurance of cold than heat. But my chief delights were the sight of the flowers, the birds, and all the gay apparel of summer . . . At length I wandered towards these mountains, and have ranged through their immense recesses, consumed by a burning passion which you alone can gratify. We may not part until you have promised to comply with my requisition. I am alone and miserable; man will not associate with me; but one as deformed and horrible as myself would not deny herself to me. My companion must be of the same species and have the same defects. This being you must create."

THE BEING finished speaking and fixed his looks upon me in the expectation of a reply. But I was bewildered, perplexed, and unable to arrange my ideas sufficiently to understand the full extent of his proposition. He continued, "You must create a female for me with whom I can live in the interchange of those sympathies necessary for my being. This you alone can do, and I demand it of you as a right which you must not refuse to concede."

The latter part of his tale had kindled anew in me the anger that had died away while he narrated his peaceful life among the cottagers, and as he said this I could no longer suppress the rage that burned within me.

"I do refuse it," I replied; "and no torture shall ever extort a consent from me. You may render me the most miserable of men, but you shall never make me base in my own eyes. Shall I create another like yourself, whose joint wickedness might desolate the world? Begone! I have answered you; you may torture me, but I will never consent."

"You are in the wrong," replied the fiend; "and instead of threatening, I am content to reason with you. I am malicious because I am miserable. Am I not shunned and hated by all mankind? You, my creator, would tear me to pieces and triumph; remember that, and tell me why I should pity man more than he pities me? You would not call it murder if you could precipitate me into one of those ice-rifts and destroy my frame, the work of your own hands. Shall I respect man when he condemns me? Let him live with me in the interchange of kindness, and instead of injury I would bestow every benefit upon him with tears of gratitude at his acceptance. But that cannot be; the human senses are insurmountable barriers to our union. Yet mine shall not be the submission of abject slavery. I will revenge my injuries; if I cannot inspire love, I will cause fear, and chiefly towards you my arch-enemy, because my creator, do I swear inextinguishable hatred. Have a care; I will work at your destruction, nor finish until I desolate your heart, so that you shall curse the hour of your birth."

A fiendish rage animated him as he said this; his face was wrinkled into contortions too horrible for human eyes to behold; but presently he calmed himself and proceeded, "I intended to reason. This passion is detrimental to me, for you do not reflect that *you* are the cause of its excess. If any being felt emotions of benevolence towards me, I should return them a hundred and a hundredfold; for that one creature's sake I would make peace with the whole kind! But I now indulge in dreams of bliss that cannot be realised. What I ask of you is reasonable and moderate; I demand a creature of another sex, but as hideous as myself; the gratification is small, but it is all that I can receive, and it shall content me. It is true, we shall be monsters, cut off from all the world; but on that account we shall be more attached to one another. Our lives will not be happy, but they will be harmless and free from the misery I now feel. Oh! My creator, make me happy; let me feel gratitude towards you for one benefit! Let me see that I excite the sympathy of some existing thing; do not deny me my request!"

I was moved. I shuddered when I thought of the possible consequences of my consent, but I felt that there was some justice in his argument. His tale and the feelings he now expressed proved him to be a creature of fine sensations, and did I not as his maker owe him all the portion of happiness that it was in my power to bestow? He saw my change of feeling and continued, "If you consent, neither you nor any other human being shall ever see us again; I will go to the vast wilds of South America. My food is not that of man; I do not destroy the lamb and the kid to glut my appetite; acorns and berries afford me sufficient nourishment. My companion will be of the same nature as myself and will be content with the same fare. We shall make our bed of dried leaves; the sun will shine on us as on man and will ripen our food. The picture I present to you is peaceful and human, and you must feel that you could deny it only in the wantonness of power and cruelty. Pitiless as you have been towards me, I now see compassion in your eyes; let me seize the favourable moment and persuade you to promise what I so ardently desire. . . I swear to you, by the earth which I inhabit, and by you that made me, that with the companion you bestow I will quit the neighbourhood of man and dwell, as it may chance, in the most savage of places. My evil passions will have fled, for I shall meet with sympathy! My life will flow quietly away, and in my dying moments I shall not curse my maker."

His words had a strange effect upon me. I compassionated him and sometimes felt a wish to console him, but when I looked upon him, when I saw the filthy mass that moved and talked, my heart sickened and my feelings were altered to those of horror and hatred.

ROBERT BARR (1850–1912)

An Alpine Divorce (1887)

This was a story found in an old collection from a charity shop, and yet it hardly seems old at all. The plot is very like something from Roald Dahl both in the use of the married couple and the ending.

IN SOME natures there are no half-tones; nothing but raw primary colours. John Bodman was a man who was always at one extreme or the other. This probably would have mattered little had he not married a wife whose nature was an exact duplicate of his own.

Doubtless there exists in this world precisely the right woman for any given man to marry, and vice versa; but when you consider that a human being has the opportunity of being acquainted with only a few hundred people, and out of the few hundred that there are but a dozen or less whom he knows intimately, and, out of the dozen, one or two friends at most, it will easily be seen, when we remember the number of millions who inhabit this world, that probably since the earth was created the right man has never yet met the right woman. The mathematical chances are all against such a meeting, and this is the reason that divorce courts exist. Marriage at best is but a compromise, and if two people happen to be united who are of an uncompromising nature there is trouble.

In the lives of these two young people there was no middle distance. The result was bound to be either love or hate, and in the case of Mr. and Mrs. Bodman it was hate of the most bitter and arrogant kind.

In some parts of the world incompatibility of temper is considered a just cause for obtaining a divorce, but in England no such subtle distinction is made, and so, until the wife became criminal, or the man became both criminal and cruel, these two were linked together by a bond that only death could sever. Nothing can be worse than this state of things, and the matter was only made the more hopeless by the fact that Mrs. Bodman lived a blameless life, and her husband was no worse, but rather better, than the majority of men. Perhaps, however, that statement held only up to a certain point, for John Bodman had reached a

state of mind in which he resolved to get rid of his wife at all hazards. If he had been a poor man he would probably have deserted her, but he was rich, and a man cannot freely leave a prospering business because his domestic life happens not to be happy.

When a man's mind dwells too much on any one subject, no one can tell just how far he will go. The mind is a delicate instrument, and even the law recognises that it is easily thrown from its balance. Bodman's friends – for he had friends – claim that his mind was unhinged; but neither his friends nor his enemies suspected the truth of the episode, which turned out to be the most important, as it was the most ominous, event in his life.

Whether John Bodman was sane or insane at the time he made up his mind to murder his wife will never be known, but there was certainly craftiness in the method he devised to make the crime appear the result of an accident. Nevertheless, cunning is often a quality in a mind that has gone wrong.

Mrs. Bodman well knew how much her presence afflicted her husband, but her nature was as relentless as his, and her hatred of him was, if possible, more bitter than his hatred of her. Wherever he went she accompanied him, and perhaps the idea of murder would never have occurred to him if she had not been so persistent in forcing her presence upon him at all times and on all occasions. So, when he announced to her that he intended to spend the month of July in Switzerland, she said nothing, but made her preparations for the journey. On this occasion he did not protest, as was usual with him, and so to Switzerland this silent couple departed.

There is an hotel near the mountain-tops, which stands on a ledge over one of the great glaciers. It is a mile and a half above the level of the sea, and it stands alone, reached by a toilsome road that zigzags up the mountain for six miles. There is a wonderful view of snow-peaks and glaciers from the verandahs of this hotel, and in the neighbourhood are many picturesque walks to points more or less dangerous.

John Bodman knew the hotel well, and in happier days he had been intimately acquainted with the vicinity. Now that the thought of murder arose in his mind, a certain spot two miles distant from this inn continually haunted him. It was a point of view overlooking everything, and its extremity was protected by a low and crumbling wall. He arose one morning at four o'clock, slipped unnoticed out of the hotel, and went to this point, which was locally named the Hanging Outlook. His memory had served him well. It was exactly the spot, he said to himself. The mountain which rose up behind it was wild and precipitous. There were no inhabitants near to overlook the place. The distant hotel was hidden by a shoulder of rock. The mountains on the other side of the valley were too far away to make it possible for any casual tourist or native to see what was going on on the Hanging Outlook. Far down in the valley the only town in view seemed like a collection of little toy houses.

One glance over the crumbling wall at the edge was generally sufficient for a visitor of even the strongest nerves. There was a sheer drop of more than a mile straight down, and at the distant bottom were jagged rocks and stunted trees that looked, in the blue haze, like shrubbery.

"This is the spot," said the man to himself, "and tomorrow morning is the time."

John Bodman had planned his crime as grimly and relentlessly, and as coolly, as ever he had concocted a deal on the Stock Exchange. There was no thought in his mind of mercy for his unconscious victim. His hatred had carried him far.

The next morning, after breakfast, he said to his wife: "I intend to take a walk in the mountains. Do you wish to come with me?"

"Yes," she answered briefly.

"Very well, then," he said; "I shall be ready at nine o'clock."

"I shall be ready at nine o'clock," she repeated after him.

At that hour they left the hotel together, to which he was shortly to return alone. They spoke no word to each other on their way to the Hanging Outlook. The path was practically level, skirting the mountains, for the Hanging Outlook was not much higher above the sea than the hotel.

John Bodman had formed no fixed plan for his procedure when the place was reached. He resolved to be guided by circumstances. Now and then a strange fear arose in his mind that she might cling to him and possibly drag him over the precipice with her. He found himself wondering whether she had any premonition of her fate, and one of his reasons for not speaking was the fear that a tremor in his voice might possibly arouse her suspicions. He resolved that his action should be sharp and sudden, that she might have no choice either to help herself or to drag him with her. Of her screams in that desolate region he had no fear. No one could reach the spot except from the hotel, and no one that morning had left the house, even for an expedition to the glacier – one of the easiest and most popular trips from the place.

Curiously enough, when they came within sight of the Hanging Outlook, Mrs. Bodman stopped and shuddered. Bodman looked at her through the narrow slits of his veiled eyes, and wondered again if she had any suspicion. No one can tell, when two people walk closely together, what unconscious communication one mind may have with another.

"What is the matter?" he asked gruffly. "Are you tired?"

"John," she cried, with a gasp in her voice, calling him by his Christian name for the first time in years, "don't you think that if you had been kinder to me at first things might have been different?"

"It seems to me," he answered, not looking at her, "that it is rather late in the day for discussing that question."

"I have much to regret," she said quaveringly. "Have you nothing?"

"No," he answered.

"Very well," replied his wife, with the usual hardness returning to her voice. "I was merely giving you a chance. Remember that."

Her husband looked at her suspiciously.

"What do you mean?" he asked, "giving me a chance? I want no chance nor anything else from you. A man accepts nothing from one he hates. My feeling towards you is, I imagine, no secret to you. We are tied together, and you have done your best to make the bondage insupportable."

"Yes," she answered, with her eyes on the ground, "we are tied together – we are tied together!"

She repeated these words under her breath as they walked the few remaining steps to the Outlook. Bodman sat down upon the crumbling wall. The woman dropped her alpenstock* on the rock, and walked nervously to and fro, clasping and unclasping her hands. Her husband caught his breath as the terrible moment drew near.

"Why do you walk about like a wild animal?" he cried. "Come here and sit down beside me, and be still."

She faced him with a light he had never before seen in her eyes – a light of insanity and of hatred.

"I walk like a wild animal," she said, "because I am one. You spoke a moment ago of your hatred of me; but you are a man, and your hatred is nothing to mine. Bad as you are, much as you wish to break the bond which ties us together, there are still things which I know you would not stoop to. I know there is no thought of murder in your heart, but there is in mine. I will show you, John Bodman, how much I hate you."

The man nervously clutched the stone beside him, and gave a guilty start as she mentioned murder.

"Yes," she continued, "I have told all my friends in England that I believed you intended to murder me in Switzerland."

"Good God!" he cried. "How could you say such a thing?"

"I say it to show how much I hate you – how much I am prepared to give for revenge. I have warned the people at the hotel, and when we left two men followed us. The proprietor tried to persuade me not to accompany you. In a few moments those two men will come in sight of

---

* alpenstock: long stick, pointed with iron, used in climbing

the Outlook. Tell them, if you think they will believe you, that it was an accident."

The mad woman tore from the front of her dress shreds of lace and scattered them around.

Bodman started up to his feet, crying, "What are you about?" But before he could move toward her she precipitated herself over the wall, and went shrieking and whirling down the awful abyss.

The next moment two men came hurriedly round the edge of the rock and found the man standing alone. Even in his bewilderment he realised that if he told the truth he would not be believed.

HSI-CHÜN

The Lament of Hsi-Chün
(translated from the Chinese by Arthur Waley)

It is difficult not to hear the human voice and feel the sadness and isolation of this Chinese lady expressed more than 2000 years ago. The translator explains that about 110 BC she was married, for political reasons, to an old Asian King. They had no common language and so couldn't communicate and they only saw each other once or twice a year. This is a cry of isolation which — like the Chinese poem earlier in this section and the Emily Dickinson poems — is written in simple but vivid and memorable phrases.

MY PEOPLE have married me
In a far corner of Earth;
Sent me away to a strange land,
To the King of the Wu-sun.
A tent is my house
Of felt are my walls;
Raw flesh my food
With mare's milk to drink.
Always thinking of my own country,
My heart sad within.
Would I were a yellow stork
And could fly to my old home!

March 13th 1832

A
Hint to Husbands & Wives
Or, an entertaining Dialogue between a Man & his Wife in this neighbourhood concerning Housekeeping.

Husband. BRING me my holiday clothes, and give me half-a-crown to put in my pocket that I may appear like another man, for I have got an invitation card to spend this evening at a Free and Easy.

Wife.—Why, Charles, I have but one sixpence in the world, and I wonder how you can expect me to have more, when you know I am paying weekly for the childrens' shoes, and you know I buy every thing to the best advantage

Husband.—What! only sixpence left, and I bring you twenty shillings a week, whilst many of our neighbours bring home only fifteen; besides we have but five children, and the two youngest cannot destroy a great deal

Wife.—Well, my dear, I do not wish to contradict you, as it often brings on strife, but as I know you to be a man that will hear reason, I will reckon things up to you, that you may know what I have to pay.

Husband.—Well, Sally, it is what I never did do, but as it is your proposal, begin your reckoning, and I shall convince you that you have about five shillings to spare.

Wife.—Well, Charles, in the first place there is 8 quartern loaves, that is 4s. 8d.,—then there is 9lb. of meat which is 4s. 6d., that is only 1lb. per day, and 3lb. for Sunday.

Husband.—Well, my dear, that is not half of twenty shillings yet.

Wife.—Stop, Charles, you have not half the expences yet: There is 1s. 6d. per week at least for potatoes & greens, and 1½d for pot-herbs, tea 1s., sugar 1s. 3d., candles 6d., soap 7d., starch and blue 1d., wood, 2d., herrings 2d., which you will have on a Sunday morning, and your tobacco 9½d., and 2 half-pints of beer which is all I allow myself during the week.

Husband.—Well, Sally, I find all these articles amount to 15s. and 6d. it is as I expected, that you would have four shillings and sixpence to spare.

Wife.—But stop my dear, then there is 3s. for rent, and firing 1s. 6d., which makes just the money.

Husband.—Oh! the rent and firing, I had quite forgot.

Wife.—Now, Charles, let me ask you what is to cloathe us, and buy other little articles which I have not mentioned.

Husband.—Say no more, take back my holiday clothes, bring me pen, ink, and paper, that I may publish the house expences as a hint to others, being certain that no person knows what money it takes, except those that have the laying of it out.

J. Catnach, Printer, 2, Monmouth-court, 7 Dials.

A broadsheet produced in 1832.

DEATH AND GLORY

ANON

The Killing of the Monster and his Mother
(from *Beowulf*, 8th century, translated by Kevin Crossley-Holland)

This Anglo-Saxon poem was part of the oral tradition of telling stories of great deeds by great men. The original looks strange with the odd letters which we have lost through time. The lines printed here, equivalent to the opening of the extract, show the way that these poems used alliteration, repeating a particular initial letter through a line. Two additional letters are used: Ð (eth) and þ (thorn) for the "th" sound.

> Ðā cōm of mōre   under mist-hleoþum
> Grendel gongan,   Godes yrre bær;
> mynte sē mān-scaðǎ   manna cynnes
> sumne besyrwan   in sele þām hēan.
> Wōd under wolcnum,   tō þæs þe hē win-reced,

If you try to say it you may notice the much more "physical" sound of the lines created by those hard consonants. The story is both dramatic and moving with Beowulf finally killed, a heroic figure, but always vulnerably human. In the extract, Beowulf and his men, from the Swedish tribe the Geats, have gone to the aid of the Danes who are being terrorised by the monster Grendel. Here, in the dark, the Geats wait in the Danes' Hall, Heorot.

THROUGH THE dark night a darker shape slid. A sinister figure shrithed down from the moors, over high shoulders, sopping tussocks, over sheep-runs, over gurgling streams. It shrithed towards the timbered hall, huge and hairy and slightly stooping. Its long arms swung loosely.

One man was snoring, one mumbling, one coughing; all the Geats guarding Heorot had fallen asleep – all except one, one man watching.

For a moment the shape waited outside the hall. It cocked an ear. It began to quiver. Its hair bristled. Then it grasped the great ring-handle and swung open the door, the mouth of Heorot. It lunged out of the darkness and into the circle of dim candlelight, it took a long stride across the patterned floor.

Through half-closed eyes Beowulf was watching, and through barred teeth he breathed one word. "Grendel." The name of the monster, the loathsome syllables.

Grendel saw the knot of sleeping warriors and his eyes shone with an unearthly light. He lurched towards the nearest man, a brave Geat called Leofric, scooped him up and, with one ghastly claw, choked the scream in his throat. Then the monster ripped him apart, bit into his body, drank the blood from his veins, devoured huge pieces; within one minute he had swallowed the whole man, even his feet and hands.

Still the Geats slept. The air in Heorot was thick with their sleep, thicker still with death and the stench of the monster.

Grendel slobbered spittle and blood; his first taste of flesh only made him more ravenous. He wheeled round towards Beowulf, stooped, reached out for him, and Beowulf . . .

Beowulf leaped up and stayed the monster's outstretched arm.

Grendel grunted and pulled back. And at that sound, all the other Geats were instantly awake. They grabbed their swords, they backed off, they shouted for Beowulf.

Grendel tried to break free but Beowulf held him fast. The monster snorted and tugged, he could feel his fingers cracking in the Geat's grip.

Now the great room boomed. Clang and clatter shattered the night-silence as Beowulf and Grendel lurched to and fro in their deathly tug-of-war. Tables and mead-benches were overturned, Grendel roared and snarled, and in the outbuildings Danes woke and listened in the darkness.

When the Geats saw that Grendel could not escape Beowulf's grip, they surrounded him and slashed at him with their swords.

Heorot flashed with battle-lights. Those warriors did not know that no kind of weapon, not even the finest iron on earth, could wound their enemy. His skin was like old rind, tough and almost hard; he had woven a secret spell against every kind of battle-blade.

Now Beowulf twisted Grendel's right arm behind his neck. He locked it and turned it, slowly he turned it, putting terrible pressure on Grendel's shoulder.

The monster bellowed and dropped to one knee. He jerked and his whole body shuddered and trembled. With superhuman strength he jerked again as he tried to escape Beowulf's grip, he jerked and all at once, his right shoulder ripped. A ghastly tearing of muscle and sinew and flesh; a spurting of hot blood: the monster's arm came apart from his body. Grendel howled. He staggered away from Beowulf, and reeled out of the hall.

The Geats cheered and shouted; they hugged one another; they converged on Beowulf.

Beowulf was gasping. "I wanted to throttle him . . ."

"He's finished!" roared one Geat.

". . . here and now."

"Done for!" shouted another.

"I couldn't hold him . . . not strong enough . . ."

"Wherever he goes," said a third companion, "death goes with him."

"I've done as I said," Beowulf panted, "and avenged Leofric."

Until that very moment, the Geats were not aware that they had lost one of their companions. They listened as Beowulf told them what had happened when Grendel first came to the hall; and all their joy at the monster's death turned to anger and gloom at the fate of Leofric.

"Look at this hand!" muttered one man.

"Each nail like steel."

"Each claw, I'd say."

"Ten terrifying spikes."

"Hand, arm and shoulder."

"No man can withstand Beowulf . . ."

". . . and no monster neither."

Beowulf raised a hand and the Geats fell silent. "Hang it up!" Beowulf said. "Stick it up outside the door, under the gable. And then give Hrothgar news of my victory."

Beowulf's companions hastened to do as he asked. One man climbed onto another's shoulders just outside the great door, and by guttering candlelight secured Grendel's grasp, blood-stained and battle-hardened, under the gable. Two others found brands at the hearth, rekindled them in the embers, and headed for the outbuildings.

Within a few minutes the first Danish warriors hurried into the hall. Others followed on their heels and then, at dawn, as the eastern sky turned pale green mackerel, the king himself proceeded to the hall on his old unsteady legs, supported by Wealhtheow, his queen. He paused at the door, marvelled at the monster's grasp, and then embraced Beowulf.

"This hall Heorot," Beowulf said, "I return it to you. Once again you can call it your own."

"I'd lost hope," Hrothgar said. "Lost all belief that anyone could end it, this monstrous nightmare."

"Twelve winters," said Wealhtheow.

"I kept my word," Beowulf said, "and fought hand to hand on equal terms."

"Beowulf, best of men, from this day on I will treat you like a son;

whatever I have here on this middle-earth will be yours also."

Wealhtheow looked troubled at the king's words, but she smiled and said nothing. Once more Hrothgar stepped forward and embraced Beowulf.

Word of Grendel's death quickly spread far and wide. Throughout that day hundreds of Danes converged on Heorot to stare at the monster's cruel grasp, and in the evening Hrothgar held a feast in honour of Beowulf and the Geats.

The king gave Beowulf shining rewards for killing Grendel – a stiff battle banner woven with gold thread, a helmet incised with battle scenes, a coat-of-mail and, finest of all, the huge damascened* sword that once belonged to Healfdene, the king's own father.

Then, at a sign from Hrothgar, eight horses with gold-plated bridles pranced into the hall. "This saddle," said Hrothgar, "so well cut and inlaid with precious stones, this is my own. Take it and take these horses, and make good use of them."

Finally, Hrothgar gave a gold buckle to each of the Geats who had crossed the sea with Beowulf, and decreed that gold should be paid for the life of the warrior Leofric. The warriors drank and feasted and drank again. Then the poet sang a lay, he compared Beowulf to Sigemund, the dragon-slayer. Waves of noise broke out along the benches, talk and laughter.

"As it used to be," said Hrothgar.

"And will be," said Wealhtheow. "Give rewards, Hrothgar, while you may. But remember your own sons! Leave this land, leave this Danish people to our sons when the day comes for you to die."

At the end of the evening, Hrothgar and Wealhtheow retired to their quarters, and Beowulf was conducted to a bed in the outbuildings where he could sleep alone and more peacefully; he was weary after his night's work. But all the other Danes and Geats remained in Heorot.

Benches were pushed back, the whole floor was padded with bolsters and pillows; and at each man's head, his helmet and coat-of-mail, his spear and shield, gleamed in the gloom.

Silence in the hall, dark and deeper dark, another night for men: one of the feasters sleeping in Heorot was doomed and soon to die . . .

IN THE MIDDLE of the night, two servants with flaming torches roused Beowulf from his sleep and escorted him to Hrothgar's chamber. "Aeschere!" said the king. He shook his head and his face creased, a grey grief-map. "Now Aeschere!"

"I am here," Beowulf said.

"Aeschere is dead. My dear old friend, my battle companion."

"In the hall?"

* damascened: inlaid with designs in gold or silver

"Two monsters! Just as some men have said, there are two monsters after all, rulers of the moors, rangers of the fell-country. Grendel and his mother, and it will never end."

"It will end," Beowulf said.

"She came to Heorot," said the king. "She barged into the hall, mournful and ravenous, snatched down Grendel's grasp from the gable, seized the nearest man – Aeschere! My friend!"

"Vengeance," Beowulf said.

"She just tucked him under her arm, and made off into the darkness."

"There is honour amongst monsters as there is honour amongst men. Grendel's mother came to the hall to avenge the death of her son."

"Once again, Beowulf, help may be had from you alone."

"Do not grieve," Beowulf said.

"Her lair is away and over the misty moors, at the bottom of a lake."

"Better each man should avenge his dead, as Grendel's mother has done. Your days are numbered and my days are numbered . . ."

Beowulf put a hand on the old king's arm. "He who can should win renown, fame before death. That is a warrior's best memorial in this world. I promise you, Hrothgar, that wherever she turns – honeycomb caves, mountain woods – I will hunt her down."

As soon as night eased, Beowulf's stallion, one of Hrothgar's gifts, was saddled and bridled. He left Heorot at once, accompanied by the king, his own companions and a large group of Danes.

They followed the monster's tracks through the forest and over the hills. Then they headed into little-known country, wolf-slopes, wind-swept headlands, perilous ways across boggy moors. They waded through a freezing stream that plunged from beetling crags and rushed seething through a fissure, picked their way along string-thin paths, skirted small lakes where water-demons lived; at last they came to a dismal wood, stiff with hoar-frost, standing on the edge of a precipice.

The lake lay beneath, the lair of Grendel and his gruesome mother. It was blood-stained and troubled. Whipped waves reared up and reached for the sky until the air was misty, and heaven weeped.

The Geats and Danes made their way down to the side of the water. Beowulf braced his shoulders, put on his clinking corslet, and donned his helmet, hung with chain-mail to guard his neck. Then Unferth* stepped forward.

Beowulf looked at him coldly; he had not forgotten their encounter in the hall.

"I did you a great wrong in Heorot," Unferth said. "Too much beer."

"What's past is past," Beowulf said.

---

* Unferth: when Beowulf came to Heorot, Unferth challenged his reputation and refused to believe that he could succeed where others had failed.

"You're the only man alive who would risk this fight."

"Then it's right I should risk it."

"Take my sword, Beowulf. Hrunting! It never fails."

Beowulf grasped the sword, smiled and clapped Unferth on the shoulder. Then he turned to Hrothgar. "If this monster covers me with a sheet of shining blood then look after my companions. Send my gifts to Hygelac. And give this great sword back to Unferth."

Beowulf did not even wait for an answer. He dived from the bank into the water, and one of the Geats put a horn to his lips and blew an eager battle-song.

For a whole day Beowulf stroked down through the water. Then Grendel's mother saw him heading for her lair; the sea-wolf rose to meet him, clutched at him, grabbed him, swept him down and into a great vaulted chamber, a hall underwater, untouched by water.

The Geat wrestled free of Grendel's mother; she was coated with her own filth, red-eyed and roaring. He whirled the sword Hrunting, and played terrible war-music on the monster's skull. Grendel's mother roared the louder but Beowulf saw she was unharmed.

"Useless!" he shouted. "It's useless! Or else magic spells protect her." He hurled the sword away and began to grapple with Grendel's mother.

Beowulf threw the monster to the ground. But then she tripped him, held him in a fearsome clinch and drew a dagger. Beowulf could not throw her off. Then Grendel's mother stabbed at Beowulf's heart. She stabbed again. But the cunning links of chain-mail held firm and guarded Beowulf; his corslet saved him.

Now the Geat sprang to his feet. He saw a sword, massive and double-edged, made by giants, lying in one corner of the chamber. It was so huge that only he of all men could have handled it.

Beowulf ran across the floor, gripped the ringed hilt and swung the ornamented sword – he struck Grendel's mother as she lumbered towards him. The blade slashed through her neck, smashed the vertebrae. The monster moaned and fell dead at his feet.

For a long while Beowulf leaned on the blood-stained sword; his heart was pounding. A man with the strength of thirty! Slayer of Grendel and slayer of the sea-wolf! A hero without equal in this middle-world!

Then Beowulf looked about him. He saw a recess, a small cave, and in the cave he found Grendel's body, drained of life-blood. "As a trophy," Beowulf said grimly and, with one blow, he severed the monster's head. "Your head and this massive sword."

The Geat spoke too soon. The patterned blade had begun to drip and melt like a gory icicle. Because of the venom in the monster's blood, it thawed entirely, right up to the hilt. So Beowulf grasped all that remained of it, picked up the sword Hrunting and Grendel's head, and left that vaulted chamber. He swam up through the water.

LEO TOLSTOY (1828–1910)

The Bear-Hunt (1872)
(translated from the Russian by Louise and Angus Maude)

Count Leo Tolstoy is probably best known for his very famous and very long novels, **War and Peace** *and* **Anna Karenina**. *Their fame and size may seem off-putting but they are both marvellous stories, full of action and drama. Tolstoy served in the Crimean War and his writings about that may be another perspective to add to the English ones in the final section of this book. Although born into the aristocracy he took on the life of a peasant in his later years. This story is based on what happened to Tolstoy himself when he was thirty: in later life he gave up hunting on humanitarian grounds.*

WE WERE out on a bear-hunting expedition. My comrade had shot at a bear, but only gave him a flesh-wound. There were traces of blood on the snow, but the bear had got away.

We all collected in a group in the forest, to decide whether we ought to go after the bear at once or wait two or three days till he should settle down again. We asked the peasant bear-drivers whether it would be possible to get round the bear that day.

"No. It's impossible," said an old bear-driver. "You must let the bear quiet down. In five days' time it will be possible to surround him, but if you followed him now, you would only frighten him away and he would not settle down."

But a young bear-driver began disputing with the old man, saying that it was quite possible to get round the bear now.

"On such snow as this," said he, "he won't go far, for he is a fat bear. He will settle down before evening, or, if not, I can overtake him on snow-shoes."

The comrade whom I was with was against following up the bear and advised waiting. But I said:

"We need not argue. You do as you like, but I will follow up the track

with Demyán. If we get round the bear, all right. If not, we lose nothing. It is still early and there is nothing else for us to do today."

So it was arranged.

The others went back to the sledges and returned to the village. Demyán and I took some bread and remained behind in the forest.

When they had all left us, Demyán and I examined our guns and, after tucking the skirts of our warm coats into our belts, we started off, following the bear's tracks.

The weather was fine, frosty and calm; but it was hard work snow-shoeing. The snow was deep and soft: it had not caked together at all in the forest and fresh snow had fallen the day before, so that our snow-shoes sank six inches deep in the snow, and sometimes more.

The bear's tracks were visible from a distance and we could see how he had been going; sometimes sinking in up to his belly and ploughing

up the snow as he went. At first, while under large trees, we kept in sight of his track; but when it turned into a thicket of small firs, Demyán stopped.

"We must leave the trail now," said he. "He has probably settled somewhere here. You can see by the snow that he has been squatting down. Let us leave the track and go round; but we must go quietly. Don't shout or cough, or we shall frighten him away."

Leaving the track, therefore, we turned off to the left. But when we had gone about five hundred yards, there were the bear's traces again right before us. We followed them and they brought us out on to the road. There we stopped, examining the road to see which way the bear had gone. Here and there in the snow were prints of the bear's paw, claws and all, and here and there the marks of a peasant's bark shoes. The bear had evidently gone towards the village.

As we followed the road, Demyán said: "It's no use watching the road now. We shall see where he has turned off, to right or left, by the marks in the soft snow at the side. He must have turned off somewhere, for he won't have gone on to the village."

We went along the road for nearly a mile, and then saw, ahead of us, the bear's track turning off the road. We examined it. How strange! It was a bear's track right enough, only not going from the road into the forest but from the forest on to the road! The toes were pointing towards the road.

"This must be another bear," I said.

Demyán looked at it and considered a while.

"No," said he. "It's the same one. He's been playing tricks and walked backwards when he left the road."

We followed the track, and found it really was so! The bear had gone some ten steps backwards, and then, behind a fir tree, had turned round and gone straight ahead. Demyán stopped and said: "Now we are sure to get round him. There is a marsh ahead of us and he must have settled down there. Let us go round it."

We began to make our way round through a fir thicket. I was tired out by this time, and it had become still more difficult to get along. Now I glided on to juniper bushes and caught my snow-shoes in them, now a tiny fir tree appeared between my feet, or, from want of practice, my snow-shoes slipped off; and now I came upon a stump or a log hidden by the snow. I was getting very tired and was drenched with perspiration, and I took off my fur cloak. And there was Demyán all the time, gliding along as if in a boat, his snow-shoes moving as if of their own accord, never catching against anything nor slipping off. He even took my fur and slung it over his shoulder and still kept urging me on.

We went on for two more miles and came out on the other side of the marsh. I was lagging behind. My snow-shoes kept slipping off and my feet stumbled. Suddenly Demyán, who was ahead of me, stopped and waved his arm. When I came up to him, he bent down, pointing with his hand, and whispered: "Do you see the magpie chattering above that undergrowth? It scents the bear from afar. That is where he must be."

We turned off and went on for more than another half-mile and presently we came on to the old track again. We had, therefore, been right round the bear, who was now within the track we had left. We stopped, and I took off my cap and loosened all my clothes. I was as hot as in a steam bath and as wet as a drowned rat. Demyán too was flushed, and wiped his face with his sleeve.

"Well, sir," he said, "we have done our job and now we must have a rest."

The evening glow already showed red through the forest. We took off our snow-shoes and sat down on them, and got some bread and salt out of our bags. First I ate some snow and then some bread; and the bread tasted so good, that I thought I had never in my life had any like it before. We sat there resting until it began to grow dusk, and then I asked Demyán if it was far to the village.

"Yes," he said. "It must be about eight miles. We will go on there tonight, but now we must rest. Put on your fur coat, sir, or you'll be catching cold."

Demyán flattened down the snow, and breaking off some fir branches made a bed of them. We lay down side by side, resting our heads on our arms. I do not remember how I fell asleep. Two hours later I woke up, hearing something crack.

I had slept so soundly that I did not know where I was. I looked around me. How wonderful! I was in some sort of a hall, all glittering and white with gleaming pillars, and when I looked up I saw through delicate white tracery, a vault, of raven blackness and studded with coloured lights. After a good look, I remembered that we were in the forest and that what I took for a hall and pillars, were trees covered with snow and hoar-frost, and the coloured lights were stars twinkling between the branches.

Hoar-frost had settled in the night; all the twigs were thick with it, Demyán was covered with it, it was on my fur coat, and it dropped down from the trees. I woke Demyán, and we put on our snow-shoes and started. It was very quiet in the forest. No sound was heard but that of our snow-shoes pushing through the soft snow; except when now and then a tree, cracking from the frost, made the forest resound. Only once we heard the sound of a living creature. Something rustled close to us and then rushed away. I felt sure it was the bear, but when we went to the spot whence the sound had come, we found the footmarks of hares, and saw several young aspen trees with their bark gnawed. We had startled some hares while they were feeding.

We came out on the road and followed it, dragging our snow-shoes behind us. It was easy walking now. Our snow-shoes clattered as they slid behind us from side to side of the hard-trodden road. The snow creaked under our boots and the cold hoar-frost settled on our faces like down. Seen through the branches the stars seemed to be running to meet us, now twinkling, now vanishing, as if the whole sky were on the move.

I found my comrade sleeping, but woke him up and related how we had got round the bear. After telling our peasant host to collect beaters for the morning, we had supper and lay down to sleep.

I was so tired that I could have slept on till midday if my comrade had not roused me. I jumped up and saw that he was already dressed, and busy doing something to his gun.

"Where is Demyán?" said I.

"In the forest, long ago. He has already been over the tracks you made and been back here, and now he has gone to look after the beaters."

I washed and dressed, and loaded my guns; and then we got into a sledge and started.

The sharp frost still continued. It was quiet, and the sun could not be seen. There was a thick mist above us, and hoar-frost still covered everything.

After driving about two miles along the road, as we came near the forest we saw a cloud of smoke rising from a hollow, and presently reached a group of peasants, both men and women, armed with cudgels.

We got out and went up to them. The men sat roasting potatoes and laughing and talking with the women.

Demyán was there too; and when we arrived the people got up and Demyán led them away to place them in the circle we had made the day before. They went along in single file, men and women, thirty in all. The snow was so deep that we could only see them from their waists upwards. They turned into the forest and my friend and I followed in their track.

Though they had trodden a path, walking was difficult; but, on the other hand, it was impossible to fall: it was like walking between two walls of snow.

We went on in this way for nearly half a mile, when all at once we saw Demyán coming from another direction – running towards us on his snow-shoes and beckoning us to join him. We went towards him, and he showed us where to stand. I took my place and looked round me.

To my left were tall fir trees, between the trunks of which I could see a good way, and, like a black patch just visible behind the trees, I could see a beater. In front of me was a thicket of young firs, about as high as a man, their branches weighted down and stuck together with snow. Through this copse ran a path thickly covered with snow and leading straight up to where I stood. The thicket stretched away to the right of me and ended in a small glade, where I could see Demyán placing my comrade.

I examined both my guns and considered where I had better stand. Three steps behind me was a tall fir.

"That's where I'll stand," thought I, "and then I can lean my second gun against the tree"; and I moved towards the tree, sinking up to my knees in the snow at each step. I trod the snow down, and made a clearance about a yard square to stand on. One gun I kept in my hand; the other, ready cocked, I placed leaning up against the tree. Then I unsheathed and replaced my dagger, to make sure that I could draw it easily in case of need.

Just as I had finished these preparations I heard Demyán shouting in the forest: "He's up! He's up!"

And as soon as Demyán shouted, the peasants round the circle all replied in their different voices.

"Up, up, up! Ou! Ou! Ou!" shouted the men.

"Ay! Ay! Ay!" screamed the women in high-pitched tones.

The bear was inside the circle, and as Demyán drove him on, the people all round kept shouting. Only my friend and I stood silent and motionless, waiting for the bear to come towards us. As I stood gazing and listening, my heart beat violently. I trembled, holding my gun fast.

"Now, now," I thought. "He will come suddenly. I shall aim, fire, and he will drop —"

Suddenly, to my left, but at a distance, I heard something falling on the snow. I looked between the tall fir trees, and some fifty paces off, behind the trunks, saw something big and black. I took aim and waited, thinking: "Won't he come any nearer?"

As I waited I saw him move his ears, turn, and go back; and then I caught a glimpse of the whole of him in profile. He was an immense brute. In my excitement I fired, and heard my bullet go "flop" against a tree. Peering through the smoke, I saw my bear scampering back into the circle, and disappearing among the trees.

"Well," thought I. "My chance is lost. He won't come back to me. Either my comrade will shoot him or he will escape through the line of beaters. In any case he won't give me another chance."

I reloaded my gun, however, and again stood listening. The peasants were shouting all round, but to the right, not far from where my comrade stood, I heard a woman screaming in a frenzied voice: "Here he is! Here he is! Come here, come here! Oh! Oh! Ay! Ay!"

Evidently she could see the bear. I had given up expecting him and was looking to the right at my comrade. All at once I saw Demyán with a stick in his hand, and without his snow-shoes, running along a footpath towards my friend. He crouched down beside him, pointing his stick as if aiming at something, and then I saw my friend raise his gun and aim in the same direction. Crack! He fired.

"There," thought I. "He has killed him."

But I saw that my comrade did not run towards the bear. Evidently he had missed him or the shot had not taken full effect.

"The bear will get away," I thought. "He will go back, but he won't come a second time towards me. – But what is that?"

Something was coming towards me like a whirlwind, snorting as it came, and I saw the snow flying up quite near me. I glanced straight before me, and there was the bear, rushing along the path through the thicket right at me, evidently beside himself with fear. He was hardly half a dozen paces off, and I could see the whole of him – his black chest and enormous head with a reddish patch. There he was, blundering straight at me and scattering the snow about as he came. I could see by his eyes that he did not see me, but, mad with fear, was rushing blindly along, and his path led him straight at the tree under which I was standing. I raised my gun and fired. He was almost upon me now and I saw that I had missed. My bullet had gone past him, and he did not even hear me fire, but still came headlong towards me. I lowered my gun and fired again, almost touching his head. Crack! I had hit, but not killed him!

He raised his head and, laying his ears back, came at me, showing his teeth.

I snatched at my other gun, but almost before I had touched it, he had flown at me and, knocking me over into the snow, had passed right over me.

"Thank goodness, he has left me," thought I.

I tried to rise, but something pressed me down and prevented my getting up. The bear's rush had carried him past me, but he had turned back and had fallen on me with the whole weight of his body. I felt something heavy weighing me down, and something warm above my face, and I realised that he was drawing my whole face into his mouth. My nose was already in it and I felt the heat of it, and smelt his blood. He was pressing my shoulders down with his paws so that I could not move: all I could do was to draw my head down towards my chest away from his mouth, trying to free my nose and eyes, while he tried to get his teeth into them. Then I felt that he had seized my forehead just under the hair with the teeth of his lower jaw, and the flesh below my eyes with his upper jaw, and was closing his teeth. It was as if my face were being cut with knives. I struggled to get away, while he made haste to close his

jaws like a dog gnawing. I managed to twist my face away, but he began drawing it again into his mouth.

"Now," thought I, "my end has come!"

Then I felt the weight lifted, and looking up, I saw that he was no longer there. He had jumped off me and run away.

When my comrade and Demyán had seen the bear knock me down and begin worrying me, they rushed to the rescue. My comrade, in his haste, blundered, and instead of following the trodden path, ran into the deep snow and fell down. While he was struggling out of the snow, the bear was gnawing at me. But Demyán just as he was, without a gun and with only a stick in his hand, rushed along the path shouting: "He's eating the master! He's eating the master!"

And as he ran, he called to the bear: "Oh, you idiot! What are you doing? Leave off! Leave off!"

The bear obeyed him, and leaving me ran away.

When I rose, there was as much blood on the snow as if a sheep had been killed and the flesh hung in rags above my eyes, though in my excitement I felt no pain.

My comrade had come up by this time and the other people collected round, they looked at my wound and put snow on it. But I, forgetting about my wounds, only asked: "Where's the bear? Which way has he gone?"

Suddenly I heard: "Here he is! Here he is!"

And we saw the bear again running at us. We seized our guns, but before any one had time to fire, he had run past. He had grown ferocious and wanted to gnaw me again, but seeing so many people he took fright. We saw by his track that his head was bleeding, and we wanted to follow him up; but, as my wounds had become very painful, we went instead to the town to find a doctor.

The doctor stitched up my wounds with silk, and they soon began to heal.

A month later we went to hunt that bear again, but I did not get a chance of finishing him. He would not come out of the circle, but went round and round, growling in a terrible voice.

Demyán killed him. The bear's lower jaw had been broken, and one of his teeth knocked out by my bullet.

He was a huge creature and had splendid black fur.

I had him stuffed, and he now lies in my room. The wounds on my forehead healed up so that the scars can scarcely be seen.

BRET HARTE (1839–1902)

What the Bullet Sang

*Bret Harte is best known as one of a group of American writers from the
"civilised" East coast who wrote about the wilder west in a direct language that
often involved dialect. His short stories are worth looking for (including "The
Outcast of Poker Flat"). This poem is a macabre mixture of styles and points of
view in giving a love song to a bullet.*

O JOY of creation,
   To be!
O rapture, to fly
   And be free!
Be the battle lost or won,
Though the smoke shall hide the sun,
I shall find my love, the one
   Born for me!

I shall know him where he stands
   All alone,
With the power in his hands
   Not o'erthrown;
I shall know him by his face,
By his godlike front and grace;
I shall hold him for a space
   All my own!

It is he – O my love!
   So bold!
It is I – all thy love
   Foretold!
It is I – O love, what bliss!
Dost thou answer to my kiss?
O sweetheart! what is this
   Lieth there so cold?

WILLIAM HOWARD RUSSELL (1820–1907)

The Cavalry Action at Balaklava
(from *The Times* November 14, 1854)

Russell's epitaph describes him as "the first and greatest" war correspondent and while he might not have been either his work, particularly in the Crimea, gave new status to the journalist. He described himself as "the miserable parent of a luckless tribe" and it is interesting to compare him with the war correspondents of our time. The gap between the event (October 25) and its publication might seem astonishing to us but more noticeable is the way he reports what he sees, the sense he has of his responsibility to the facts and his audience back home. The report had an enormous public impact and inspired Tennyson to write his famous poem (see page 115).

I F THE EXHIBITION of the most brilliant valour, of the excess of courage, and of a daring which would have reflected lustre on the best days of chivalry can afford full consolation for the disaster of today, we can have no reason to regret the melancholy loss which we sustained in a contest with a savage and barbarian enemy.

I shall proceed to describe, to the best of my power, what occurred under my own eyes, and to state the facts which I have heard from men whose veracity is unimpeachable, reserving to myself the exercise of the right of private judgement in making public and in suppressing the details of what occurred on this memorable day. . .

And now occurred the melancholy catastrophe which fills us all with sorrow. It appears that the Quartermaster General, Brigadier Airey, thinking that the Light Cavalry had not gone far enough in front when the enemy's horse had fled, gave an order in writing to Captain Nolan, 15th Hussars, to take to Lord Lucan, directing His Lordship "to advance" his cavalry nearer to the enemy. . . .

God forbid I should cast a shade on the brightness of his honour, but I am bound to state what I am told occurred when he reached His Lordship. I should premise that, as the Russian cavalry retired, their infantry fell back towards the head of the valley, leaving men in three of the redoubts they had taken and abandoning the fourth. They had also placed some guns on the heights over their position, on the left of the gorge. Their cavalry joined the reserves, and drew up in six solid divisions, in an oblique line, across the entrance to the gorge. Six battalions of infantry were placed behind them, and about thirty guns were drawn up along their line, while masses of infantry were also collected on the hills behind the redoubts on our right. Our cavalry had moved up to the ridge across the valley, on our left, as the ground was broken in front, and had halted in the order I have already mentioned.

When Lord Lucan received the order from Captain Nolan and had read it, he asked, we are told, "Where are we to advance to?"

Captain Nolan pointed with his finger to the line of the Russians, and said, "There are the enemy, and there are the guns, sir, before them. It is your duty to take them," or words to that effect, according to the statements made since his death.

Lord Lucan with reluctance gave the order to Lord Cardigan to advance upon the guns, conceiving that his orders compelled him to do so. The noble Earl, though he did not shrink, also saw the fearful odds against him. Don Quixote in his tilt against the windmill was not near so rash and reckless as the gallant fellows who prepared without a thought to rush on almost certain death.

It is a maxim of war that "cavalry never act without support", that "infantry should be close at hand when cavalry carry guns, as the effect is only instantaneous", and that it is necessary to have on the flank of a line of cavalry some squadrons in column, the attack on the flank being most dangerous. The only support our Light Cavalry had was the reserve of Heavy Cavalry at a great distance behind them – the infantry and guns being far in the rear. There were no squadrons in column at all, and there was a plain to charge over before the enemy's guns were reached of a mile and a half in length.

At ten past eleven our Light Cavalry Brigade rushed to the front. They numbered as follows, as well as I could ascertain:

	MEN
4th Light Dragoons	118
8th Irish Hussars	104
11th Prince Albert's Hussars	110
13th Light Dragoons	130
17th Lancers	145
Total	607 sabres

The whole brigade scarcely made one effective regiment, according to the numbers of continental armies; and yet it was more than we could spare. As they passed towards the front, the Russians opened on them from the guns in the redoubts on the right, with volleys of musketry and rifles.

They swept proudly past, glittering in the morning sun in all the pride and splendour of war. We could hardly believe the evidence of our senses! Surely that handful of men were not going to charge an army in position? Alas! it was but too true – their desperate valour knew no bounds, and far indeed was it removed from its so-called better part – discretion. They advanced in two lines, quickening their pace as they closed towards the enemy. A more fearful spectacle was never witnessed than by those who, without the power to aid, beheld their heroic countrymen rushing to the arms of death. At the distance of 1200 yards the whole line of the enemy belched forth, from thirty iron mouths, a flood of smoke and flame, through which hissed the deadly balls. Their flight was marked by instant gaps in our ranks, by dead men and horses, by steeds flying wounded or riderless across the plain. The first line was broken – it was joined by the second, they never halted or checked their speed an instant. With diminished ranks, thinned by those thirty guns, which the Russians had laid with the most deadly accuracy, with a halo of flashing steel above their heads, and with a cheer which was many a noble fellow's death cry, they flew into the smoke of the batteries; but ere they were lost from view, the plain was strewed with their bodies and with the carcasses of horses. They were exposed to an oblique fire from the batteries on the hills on both sides, as well as to a direct fire of musketry.

Through the clouds of smoke we could see their sabres flashing as they rode up to the guns and dashed between them, cutting down the gunners as they stood. The blaze of their steel, as an officer standing near me said, was "like the turn of a shoal of mackerel". We saw them riding through the guns, as I have said; to our delight we saw them returning, after breaking through a column of Russian infantry, and scattering them like chaff, when the flank fire of the battery on the hill swept them down, scattered and broken as they were. Wounded men and dismounted troopers flying towards us told the sad tale – demigods could not have done what they had failed to do. At the very moment when they were about to retreat, an enormous mass of lancers was hurled upon their flank. Colonel Shewell, of the 8th Hussars, saw the danger, and rode his few men straight at them, cutting his way through with fearful loss. The other regiments turned and engaged in a desperate encounter. With courage too great almost for credence, they were breaking their way through the columns which enveloped them, when there took place an act of atrocity without parallel in the modern warfare of civilised nations. The Russian gunners, when the storm of cavalry passed, returned to their guns. They saw their own cavalry mingled with the troopers who had just ridden over them, and to the eternal disgrace of the Russian name the miscreants poured a murderous volley of grape and canister on the mass of struggling men and horses, mingling friend and foe in one common ruin. It was as much as our Heavy Cavalry Brigade could do to cover the retreat of the miserable remnants of that band of heroes as they returned to the place they had so lately quitted in all the pride of life.

At twenty-five to twelve not a British soldier, except the dead and dying, was left in front of these bloody Muscovite guns. Our loss, as far as it could be ascertained in killed, wounded, and missing at two o'clock today, was as follows:

	Went into action strong	Returned from action	loss
4th Light Dragoons	118	39	79
8th Hussars	104	38	66
11th Hussars	110	25	85
13th Light Dragoons	130	61	69
17th Lancers	145	35	110
	607	198	409

Charge of the Light Brigade at Balaklava

ALFRED LORD TENNYSON (1809–92)

The Charge of the Light Brigade

*Alfred Lord Tennyson, the Poet Laureate, was a famous public figure of his time. This poem is sometimes seen as a public celebration of the events and Tennyson is said to have have written the poem "in a few minutes after reading the description in **The Times**". It has a grand feel to it but it's no simple response to Russell's report and it took much writing and reworking even after its initial publication in 1855. He tried to respond to criticism, to catch more clearly the ambiguities of what had happened and to extend the ideas beyond this single event. It went through some twenty different stages before emerging in the form printed here.*

I

Half a league, half a league,
Half a league onward,
All in the valley of Death
  Rode the six hundred.
"Forward, the Light Brigade!
Charge for the guns!" he said:
Into the valley of Death
  Rode the six hundred.

II

"Forward, the Light Brigade!"
Was there a man dismay'd?
Not tho' the soldier knew
  Some one had blunder'd:
Their's not to make reply,
Their's not to reason why,
Their's but to do and die;
Into the valley of Death
  Rode the six hundred.

III

Cannon to right of them,
Cannon to left of them,
Cannon in front of them
  Volley'd and thunder'd;
Storm'd at with shot and shell,
Boldly they rode and well,
Into the jaws of Death,
Into the mouth of Hell
  Rode the six hundred.

IV

Flash'd all their sabres bare,
Flash'd as they turn'd in air,
Sabring the gunners there,
Charging an army, while
  All the world wonder'd:
Plunged in the battery-smoke
Right thro' the line they broke;
Cossack and Russian
Reel'd from the sabre-stroke
  Shatter'd and sunder'd.
Then they rode back, but not,
  Not the six hundred.

V

Cannon to right of them,
Cannon to left of them,
Cannon behind them
    Volley'd and thunder'd;
Storm'd at with shot and shell,
While horse and hero fell,
They that had fought so well
Came thro' the jaws of Death,
Back from the mouth of Hell,
All that was left of them,
    Left of six hundred.

VI

When can their glory fade?
O the wild charge they made!
    All the world wonder'd.
Honour the charge they made!
Honour the Light Brigade,
    Noble six hundred!

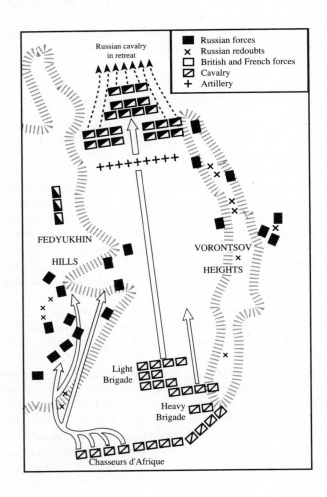

ALEXANDRE DUMAS (1802–70)

Fight to the Death (1858)

(from *Adventures In The Caucasus* translated from the French by A.E. Murch)

*Dumas was an extraordinary character, remembered now as the author of **The Three Musketeers** and **The Count of Mount Cristo**, but famous in his time for a variety of daring and not always legal exploits. The encounter described here begins slowly but builds up to a wonderful climax.*

A FTER AN HOUR and a half we reached the fortress of Shedrinskaia, where we halted to rest our horses and change our guard. This time we were given twelve, and as we rode on again, following the bank of the Terek which adjoins the road at this spot, two of our Cossacks went ahead of us, two brought up the rear, and the others galloped beside us, four on each side. To my right, as far as I could see, stretched dense thickets some three feet high, with an occasional tall tree of a different kind towering above them. To my left, the same thick bushes ran from the edge of the road to the river bank.

Suddenly a flight of partridge rose from the bushes by the river and I could not resist the chance of a shot or two, so I quickly took the bullets from my gun and slipped in a couple of light cartridges. Though the chief Cossack strongly protested that it would be risky to leave the road, I dismounted, went a dozen yards into the bushes and fired. One bird fell. "Did you see where it came down, Moynet?" I cried. "The sun's in my eyes. I know I hit one, but that's all."

"Wait a minute. I'll come and help you look," he replied, but before he could reach me I heard another shot fired a hundred yards* away. I saw a puff of smoke and at the same moment heard a bullet whistle through the upper branches of the bushes that engulfed us to the waist, and only a couple of feet away. We ran back, and saw that the bullet had hit one of the horses, breaking its foreleg high up near the body. I had

* hundred yards: 91.4 metres

already loaded my gun with fresh bullets as I ran; a Cossack was holding my mount by the bridle; I swung into the saddle and stood in my stirrups to get a wider view. What surprised me, from what I had heard of the habits of Chechen bandits, was their delay in attacking us. Usually they charge down on an enemy as soon as their first shot is fired.

At this moment we saw seven or eight men filing up from the bank of the Terek. Our Cossacks gave a cheer and raced off towards them, but then another man emerged from the thicket where he had shot at us. He made no attempt to escape, but stood his ground, brandishing his gun above his head and shouting: "*Abreck!*"

"*Abreck!*" our Cossacks shouted in reply, and reined in their horses to a standstill.

"What does that mean?" I asked Kalino.

"It means that he is sworn to seek out danger and never to turn his back to an enemy. He is challenging one of our Cossacks to single combat."

"Tell them I'll give twenty roubles to the man who accepts that challenge," I cried.

Kalino took my message to our men and there was a short silence while they looked at each other as if to choose the bravest one among them. Meanwhile, a couple of hundred yards away, the challenger was putting his horse through a complicated series of evolutions and still shouting "*Abreck!*"

"*Sacrebleu!* Pass me my carbine, Kalino," I exclaimed. "I'd love to bring him down, the arrogant rascal!"

"Don't do anything like that," he advised. "You're going to see something well worth watching. Our Cossacks are just discussing which of them is to tackle him. They've recognised him as a champion well known in these mountains. Wait! Here's one of our men coming now."

The Cossack whose horse had been shot had tried to get the animal on its feet again, but with no success. Now he was walking over to put his case before me, as leader of the expedition. According to custom he had a personal right to do so, in view of his loss. These Cossacks provide their own horses and weapons, out of their soldier's pay. When a horse is killed in action, the man's commanding officer gives him a government grant of twenty-two roubles, but since a reasonably good horse costs at least thirty the soldier will be eight roubles or more out of pocket. Our Cossack therefore claimed that he had the best right to try and win the twenty roubles I had offered. With luck, it would leave him ten roubles in hand. Had he my permission to fight the man who had wounded his horse? The suggestion seemed to me fair and just, so I expressed my approval.

Meanwhile, the mountain tribesman had been riding round us in

ever-narrowing circles and was now quite close. The eyes of our Cossacks flashed, but not one of them dishonoured the code that forbade him to shoot, once the challenge had been accepted. Their captain spoke a word or two to the man who had just left us, then said: "All right, then. Off you go, my lad!"

"But I haven't got a horse!" the Cossack replied. "Who will lend me one?" His comrades stood silent, for if a borrowed horse were killed it was doubtful whether the government would make any grant to the owner. Appreciating their difficulty, which Kalino explained to me, I jumped down from my own mount, one of the best in the cavalry stables. "Here you are," I cried. "Take mine!" Instantly the Cossack leapt into the saddle and was off.

Another Cossack came up to me. "What does he say?" I asked Kalino, who replied: "He wants to know whether, if any harm comes to his comrade, he can take his place?"

"He's in rather a hurry, it seems to me; but still, I agree."

The Cossack returned to his place and began checking his weapons as if he expected his turn to arrive at any moment. By this time, the first man was already close enough to fire, but his opponent made his horse rear so that the bullet struck it in the shoulder. His return shot carried away the Cossack's fur hat. Now they both slung their guns over their shoulders and seized their swords. The mountaineer managed his wounded horse so cleverly that, though blood was streaming down its chest, it showed no sign of weakness and responded instantly to the bridle, the pressure of its master's knees and the sound of his voice. Now the men were fighting hand to hand, and for a moment I thought our Cossack had run his enemy through, for I saw the point of the blade shine behind his back. But he had only thrust it through his jerkin. In the next few minutes it was impossible to see what was happening, but then came a pause, and slowly our Cossack slipped from his saddle. That is, his body slumped to the ground. His head, dripping with blood, was waved at us with a fierce cry of triumph, then tied to the saddle-bow of his conqueror. His horse, now riderless, circled back to join us and its stable companions.

I turned to the Cossack who had asked to be the next. He was quietly smoking his pipe, but he nodded and said: "All right! I'm going."

Then he, in turn, gave a yell of defiance to show that he now challenged the victor, and the *abreck* paused in his dance of triumph to face his new opponent. "All right," I cried to the Cossack. "Now I'll make it thirty roubles." He simply winked at me and rode away, still puffing at his pipe, but I noticed that no smoke escaped his lips and thought he must be swallowing it. Then he galloped off.

The *abreck* had had no chance to reload, and our Cossack, at a range of forty yards, shouldered his gun. We saw a puff of smoke but heard no bullet, and so concluded that his gun had misfired. By now, the mountaineer had reloaded and we saw him fire, but the Cossack made his horse swerve and so avoided the bullet, though the range was now only a few yards. Then we saw the Cossack fire again, and by the sudden jerk of the mountaineer's body we knew he had been hit. He dropped the bridle and saved himself from falling by clasping both arms round the neck of his horse. The poor animal, with no help from its rider and maddened by its own wound, bolted towards the river. We were on the point of riding off in pursuit when we saw the body of the mountaineer slipping slowly to the ground.

Our Cossack, fearing that this might be a trick and that his opponent was not really dead, circled round the fallen man, trying to see his face. But he had fallen with his face to the ground. Accordingly, ten paces away, he fired one more shot at the enemy, but the bullet was wasted. The mountain champion was dead indeed. The Cossack dismounted, drew his sword, bent over the body and a moment later stood waving the severed head, while the other Cossacks cheered wildly. He had not only won thirty roubles, he had saved the honour of his regiment and avenged his comrade.

A moment later, the mountaineer was stripped naked. The Cossack wrapped his clothes in a bundle, slung it over the back of the wounded horse, which made no attempt to escape, remounted his own horse and rode back to us. There was one question I was longing to ask him. "We all saw your gun misfire, yet you did not reload. How, then, could you manage to fire another shot?"

The Cossack laughed. "But my gun did not misfire!"

"Yes, it did!" his comrades insisted. "We all saw the smoke!"

"That's what I wanted you to think, you and that *abreck*, but really it was the smoke from my pipe. I kept it in my mouth on purpose."

"Here are your thirty roubles," I replied, counting them into his hand, "but it seems to me you're a pretty tricky customer!"

MARGARET CAVENDISH, DUCHESS OF NEWCASTLE (1624?–74)

Nature's Cook (1653)

Margaret Cavendish was a Royalist in turbulent times. She wrote scientific and philosophical pieces as well as stories, plays and poems and, as the poem may suggest, she was extravagant in her dress and behaviour. "All I desire is fame," she said. The writer Virginia Woolf, in this century, wrote of her: "What a vision of loneliness and riot the thought of Margaret Cavendish brings to mind! As if some great giant cucumber had spread itself all over the roses and carnations in the garden and choked them to death." This is a startling poem which revels in the awfulness of the menu of disease and invites you to enjoy speaking it at least. (The strange words mostly refer to diseases: "calentures" are extreme fevers — said to make sailors see fields when they looked at the sea; "megrims" are migraines.)

DEATH is the cook of Nature; and we find
Meat dressed several ways to please her mind.
Some meats she roasts with fevers, burning hot,
And some she boils with dropsies in a pot.
Some for jelly consuming by degrees,
And some with ulcers, gravy out to squeeze.
Some flesh as sage she stuffs with gouts, and pains,
Others for tender meat hangs up in chains.
Some in the sea she pickles up to keep,
Others, as brawn is soused, those in wine steep.
Some with the pox, chops flesh, and bones so small,
Of which she makes a French fricasse withal.
Some on gridirons of calentures is broiled,
And some is trodden on, and so quite spoiled.
But those are baked, when smothered they do die,
By hectic fevers some meat she doth fry.
In sweat sometimes she stews with savoury smell,
A hodge-podge of diseases tasteth well.

Brains dressed with apoplexy to Nature's wish,
Or swims with sauce of megrims in a dish.
And tongues she dries with smoke from stomachs ill,
Which as the second course she sends up still.
Then Death cuts throats, for blood-puddings to make,
And puts them in the guts, which colics rack.
Some hunted are by Death, for deer that's red.
Or stall-fed oxen, knocked on the head.
Some for bacon by Death are singed, or scaled,
Then powdered up with phlegm, and rheum that's salt.

"The Apotheosis of War" (1871) by Phassily Vereschtschagin

CRIME AND PUNISHMENT

CHARLES DICKENS (1812–70)

Sikes and Nancy
(adapted by Dickens from *Oliver Twist*)

Dickens was famous for his public readings which were much more like dramatic performances and this was a favourite piece both with the author and his audiences. Dickens created this three-chapter version himself, carefully condensing the events of five chapters and actually rewriting some parts (including the final section where, unlike the novel, events are seen through the eyes of Sikes himself). His own copy of this version is covered by underlinings, double underlinings and comments — it's a playscript waiting to be performed. Some of Dickens's underlinings — no doubt to remind him of emphases or gestures — are indicated here by italics.

Chapter I

FAGIN THE RECEIVER of stolen goods was up, betimes, one morning, and waited impatiently for the appearance of his new associate, Noah Claypole, otherwise Morris Bolter; who at length presented himself, and, cutting a monstrous slice of bread, commenced a voracious assault on the breakfast.

"Bolter, *Bolter*."

"Well, here I am. What's the matter? Don't yer ask me to do anything till I have done eating. That's a great fault in this place. Yer never get time enough over yer meals."

"You can talk as you eat, can't you?"

"Oh yes, I can talk. I get on better when I talk. *Talk away*. Yer won't interrupt me."

There seemed, indeed, no great fear of anything interrupting him, as he had evidently sat down with a determination to do a deal of business.

"I want you, Bolter," *leaning over the table*, "to do a piece of work for me, my dear, that needs great care and caution."

"I say, don't yer go a-shoving me into danger, yer know. That don't suit me, that don't; and so I tell yer."

"There's not the smallest danger in it – not the very smallest; it's only to *dodge a woman.*"

"An old woman?"

"A young one."

"I can do that pretty well. I was a regular sneak when I was at school. What am I to dodge her for? Not to –"

"Not to do anything, but tell me where she goes, who she sees, and, if possible, what she says; to remember the street, if it is a street, or the house, if it is a house; and to bring me back all the information you can."

"What'll yer give me?"

"If you do it well, a pound, my dear. One pound. And that's what I never gave yet, for any job of work where there wasn't valuable consideration to be got."

"Who is she?"

"One of us."

"Oh Lor! Yer doubtful of her, are yer?"

"She has found out some new friends, my dear, and I must know who they are."

"I see. Ha! ha! ha! I'm your man. Where is she? Where am I to wait for her? Where am I to go?"

"All that, my dear, you shall hear from me. I'll point her out at the proper time. You keep ready, in the clothes I have got here for you, and leave the rest to me."

That night, and the next, and the next again, the spy sat booted and equipped in the disguise of a carter: ready to turn out at a word from Fagin. Six nights passed, and on each, Fagin came home with a disappointed face, and briefly intimated that it was not yet time. On the seventh he returned exultant. It was Sunday Night.

"She goes abroad tonight," said Fagin, "and on the right errand, I'm sure; for she has been alone all day, and the man she is afraid of will not be back much before daybreak. Come with me! Quick!"

They left the house, and, stealing through a labyrinth of streets, arrived at length before a public house. It was past eleven o'clock, and the door was closed; but it opened softly as Fagin gave a low whistle. They entered, without noise.

Scarcely venturing to whisper, but substituting dumb show for words, Fagin pointed out a pane of glass high in the wall to Noah, and signed to him to climb up, on a piece of furniture below it, and observe the person in the adjoining room.

"Is that the woman?"

Fagin nodded "yes".

"I can't see her face well. She is looking down, and the candle is behind her."

"Stay there." He signed to the lad, who had opened the house-door to them; who withdrew – entered the room adjoining, and, under pretence of snuffing the candle, moved it in the required position; then he spoke to the girl, causing her to raise her face.

"I see her now!"

"Plainly?"

"I should know her among a thousand."

The spy descended, the room-door opened, and the girl came out. Fagin drew him behind a small partition, and they held their breath as she passed within a few feet of their place of concealment, and emerged by the door at which they had entered.

"*After her!* To the *left*. Take the left hand, and keep on the other side. *After her!*"

The spy darted off; and, by the light of the street lamps, saw the girl's retreating figure, already at some distance before him. He advanced as near as he considered prudent, and kept on the opposite side of the street. *She looked nervously round.* She seemed to gather courage as she advanced, and to walk with a steadier and firmer step. The spy preserved the same relative distance between them, and followed.

Chapter II

THE CHURCHES chimed three quarters past eleven, as the two figures emerged on London Bridge. The young woman advanced with a swift and rapid step, and looked about her as though in quest of some expected object; the young man, who slunk along in the deepest shadow he could find, and, at some distance, accommodated his pace to hers: stopping when she stopped: and as she moved again, creeping stealthily on: but never allowing himself, in the ardour of his pursuit, to gain upon her. Thus, they crossed the bridge, from the Middlesex to the Surrey shore, when the woman, disappointed in her anxious scrutiny of the foot-passengers, turned back. The movement was sudden; but the man was not thrown off his guard by it; for, shrinking into one of the recesses which surmount the piers of the bridge, and leaning over the parapet the better to conceal his figure, he suffered her to pass. When she was about the same distance in advance as she had been before, he slipped quietly down, and followed her again. At nearly the centre of the bridge she stopped. He stopped.

It was a very dark night. The day had been unfavourable, and at that hour and place there were few people stirring. Such as there were, hurried past: possibly without seeing, certainly without noticing, either the woman, or the man. Their appearance was not attractive of such of

London's destitute population, as chanced to take their way over the bridge that night; and they stood there in silence: neither speaking nor spoken to.

The girl had taken a few turns to and fro – closely watched by her hidden observer – *when the heavy bell of St. Paul's tolled for the death of another day. Midnight had come upon the crowded city. Upon the palace, the night-cellar, the jail, the madhouse: the chambers of birth and death, of health and sickness, upon the rigid face of the corpse and the calm sleep of the child.*

A young lady, accompanied by a grey-haired gentleman, alighted from a hackney-carriage. They had scarcely set foot upon the pavement of the bridge, when the girl started, and joined them.

"*Not here!* I am afraid to speak to you here. Come away – out of the public road – down the steps yonder!"

The steps to which she pointed, were those which, on the Surrey bank, and on the same side of the bridge as Saint Saviour's Church, form a landing-stairs from the river. To this spot the spy hastened unobserved; and after a moment's survey of the place, he began to descend.

These stairs are a part of the bridge; they consist of three flights. Just below the end of the second, going down, the stone wall on the left terminates in an ornamental pilaster* facing towards the Thames. At this point the lower steps widen: so that a person turning that angle of the wall, is necessarily unseen by any others on the stairs who chance to be above, if only a step. The spy looked hastily round, when he reached this point; and as there seemed no better place of concealment, and as the tide being out there was plenty of room, he slipped aside, with his back to the pilaster, and there waited: pretty certain that they would come no lower down.

So tardily went the time in this lonely place, and so eager was the spy, that he was on the point of emerging from his hiding-place, and regaining the road above, when he heard the sound of footsteps, and directly afterwards of voices almost close at his ear.

He drew himself straight upright against the wall, and listened attentively.

"This is far enough," *said a voice, which was evidently that of the gentleman.* "I will not suffer the young lady to go any further. Many people would have distrusted you too much to have come even so far, but you see I am willing to humour you."

"To humour me!" *cried the voice of the girl* whom he had followed. "You're considerate, indeed, sir. To humour me! Well, well, it's no matter."

"Why, for what purpose can you have brought us to this strange place? Why not have let me speak to you, above there, where it is light,

---

* pilaster: square or rectangular column of stone; in this instance, part of a bridge

and there is something stirring, instead of bringing us to this dark and dismal hole?"

"I told you before, that I was afraid to speak to you there. I don't know why it is," *said the girl shuddering*, "but I have such a fear and dread upon me tonight that I can hardly stand."

"A fear of what?"

"I scarcely know of what – I wish I did. Horrible thoughts of *death* – and *shrouds* with *blood* upon them – and a fear that has made me burn as if I was on fire – have been upon me all day. I was reading a book tonight, to while the time away, and the same things came into the print."

"Imagination!"

"No imagination. I swear I saw '*coffin*' written in every page of the book in large black letters, – aye, and they carried one close to me, in the streets tonight."

"There is nothing unusual in that. They have passed me often."

"*Real ones*. This was not."

"Pray speak to her kindly," said the young lady to the grey-haired gentleman. "Poor creature! She seems to need it."

"Bless you, miss, for that! Your haughty religious people would have held their heads up to see me as I am tonight, and would have preached of flames and vengeance. Oh, dear lady, why ar'n't those who claim to be God's own folks, as gentle and as kind to us poor wretches as you!"

"You were not here last Sunday night, girl, as you appointed."

"I couldn't come. I was kept by force."

"By whom?"

"*Bill – Sikes* – him that I told the young lady of before."

"You were not suspected of holding any communication with anybody on the subject which has brought us here tonight, I hope?"

"No," replied the girl, shaking her head. "It's not very easy for me to leave him unless he knows why; I couldn't have seen the lady when I did, but that I gave him a drink of *laudanum* before I came away."

"Did he awake before you returned?"

"No; and neither he nor any of them suspect me."

"Good. Now listen to me. I am Mr. Brownlow, this young lady's friend. I wish you, in this young lady's interest, and for her sake, to deliver up Fagin."

"Fagin! I will not do it! I will never do it! Devil that he is, and worse than devil as he has been to me, as my Teacher in all Devilry, I will never do it."

"Why?"

"For the reason that, bad life as he has led, I have led a bad life too; for the reason that there are many of us who have kept the same courses together, and I'll not turn upon them, who might – any of them – have turned upon me, but didn't, bad as they are. Last, for the reason – (*how can I say it with the young lady here!*) – that, among them, there is one – *this Bill – this Sikes* – the most desperate of all – *that I can't leave*. Whether it is God's wrath for the wrong I have done, I don't know, but I am drawn back to him through everything, and I should be, I believe, if I knew that I was to *die* by his hand!''

"But, put one man – not him – not one of the gang – the one man Monks into my hands, and leave him to me to deal with.''

"What if he turns against the others?''

"I promise you that, in that case, there the matter shall rest; they shall go scot free.''

"Have I the lady's promise for that?''

"You have,'' replied Rose Maylie, the young lady.

"I have been a liar, and among liars from a little child, but I will take your words.''

After receiving an assurance from both, that she might safely do so, she proceeded in a voice so low that it was often difficult for the listener to discover even the purport of what she said, to describe the means by which this one man Monks might be found and taken. But nothing would have induced her to compromise one of her own companions; little reason though she had, poor wretch! to spare them.

"Now,'' said the gentleman, when she had finished, "you have given us most valuable assistance, young woman, and I wish you to be the better for it. What can I do to serve you?''

"Nothing.''

"You will not persist in saying that; think now; take time. Tell me.''

"Nothing, sir. You can do nothing to help me. I am past all hope.''

"You put yourself beyond the pale of hope. The past has been a dreary waste with you, of youthful energies mis-spent, and such treasures lavished, as the Creator bestows but once and never grants again, but, *for the future, you may hope*! I do not say that it is in our power to offer you peace of heart and mind, for that must come as you seek it; but a quiet asylum, either in England, or, if you fear to remain here, in some foreign country, it is not only within the compass of our ability but our most anxious wish to secure you. Before the dawn of morning, before this river wakes to the first glimpse of daylight, you shall be placed as entirely beyond the reach of your former associates, and leave as complete an absence of all trace behind you, as if you were to disappear from the earth this moment. Come! I would not have you go back to exchange one word with any old companion, or take one look at any old haunt. Quit them all, while there is time and opportunity!''

"She will be persuaded now,'' cried the young lady.

"I fear not, my dear."

"*No, sir – no, miss.* I am chained to my old life. I *loathe* and *hate* it, but I cannot *leave* it. – When ladies as young and good, as happy and beautiful as you, miss, give away your hearts, love will carry even you all lengths. When such as I, who have no certain roof but the coffin-lid, and no friend in sickness or death but the hospital-nurse, set our rotten hearts on any man, who can hope to cure us! – This fear comes over me again. I must go home. Let us part. I shall be watched or seen. *Go! Go!* If I have done you any service, all I ask is, leave me, and let me go my way alone."

"Take this purse," cried the young lady. "Take it for my sake, that you may have some resource in an hour of need and trouble."

"*No!* I have not done this for *money. Let me have that to think of.* And yet – give me something that you have worn – I should like to have something – *no, no,* not a *ring,* they'd rob me of that – your *gloves* or *handkerchief* – anything that I can keep, as having belonged to you. There. *Bless you! God bless you! Good-night, good-night!*"

The agitation of the girl, and the apprehension of some discovery which would subject her to violence, seemed to determine the gentleman to leave her. The sound of retreating footsteps followed, and the voices ceased.

After a time Nancy ascended to the street. The spy remained on his post for some minutes, and then, *after peeping out,* to make sure that he was unobserved, darted away, and made for Fagin's house as fast as his legs would carry him.

Chapter III

IT WAS nearly two hours before daybreak; that time which in the autumn of the year, may be truly called the dead of night; when the streets are silent and deserted; when even sound appears to slumber, and profligacy and riot have staggered home to dream; it was at this still and silent hour, that Fagin sat in his old lair. Stretched upon a mattress on the floor, lay Noah Claypole, otherwise Morris Bolter, fast asleep. Towards him the old man sometimes directed his eyes for an instant, and then brought them back again to the wasting candle.

He sat without changing his attitude, or appearing to take the smallest heed of time, until the door-bell rang. He crept upstairs, and presently returned accompanied by a man muffled to the chin, who carried a bundle under one arm. Throwing back his outer coat, the man displayed the *burly frame of Sikes, the house-breaker.*

"*There!*" laying the bundle on the table. "Take care of that, and do the most you can with it. It's been trouble enough to get. I thought I should have been here three hours ago."

Fagin laid his hand upon the bundle, and locked it in the cupboard. But he did not take *his eyes off the robber, for an instant.*

"Wot now?" cried Sikes. "Wot do you look at a man, like that, for?"

Fagin raised his right hand, and shook his trembling forefinger in the air.

"Hallo!" *feeling in his breast.* "He's gone mad. I must look to myself here."

"No, no, it's not – you're not the person, Bill. I've no – no fault to find with you."

"Oh! you haven't, haven't you?" *passing a pistol into a more convenient pocket.* "That's lucky – for one of us. Which one that is, don't matter."

"I've got that to tell you, Bill, will make you worse than me."

"Aye? Tell away! Look sharp, or Nance will think I'm lost."

"*Lost!* She has pretty well settled that, in her own mind, already."

He looked, perplexed, into the old man's face, and reading no satisfactory explanation of the riddle there, clenched his coat collar in his huge hand and shook him soundly.

"Speak, will you? Or if you don't, it shall be for want of breath. Open your mouth and say wot you've got to say. Out with it, you *thundering, blundering, wondering* old *cur*, out with it!"

"Suppose that lad that's lying there – " Fagin began.

Sikes turned round to where Noah was sleeping, as if he had not previously observed him. "Well?"

"Suppose that lad was to peach – to blow upon us all. Suppose that lad was to do it, of his own fancy – not grabbed, tried, earwigged by the parson and brought to it on bread and water – but of his own fancy; to please his own taste; stealing out at nights to do it. Do you hear me? Suppose he did all this, what then?"

"What then? If he was left alive till I came, I'd grind his skull under the iron heel of my boot into as many grains as there are hairs upon his head."

"What if *I* did it! *I*, that know so much, and could hang so many besides myself!"

"I don't know. I'd do something in the jail that 'ud get me put in irons; and, if I was tried along with you, I'd fall upon you with them in the open court, and beat your brains out afore the people. I'd smash your head as if a loaded waggon had gone over it."

Fagin looked hard at the robber; and, motioning him to be silent, stooped over the bed upon the floor, and shook the sleeper to rouse him.

"Bolter! Bolter! *Poor lad!*" said Fagin, looking up with an expression of

devilish anticipation, and speaking slowly and with marked emphasis. "*He's tired* – tired with watching for *her* so long – watching for *her*, Bill."

"Wot d'ye mean?"

Fagin made no answer, but bending over the sleeper again, hauled him into a sitting posture. When his assumed name had been repeated several times, Noah rubbed his eyes, and, giving a heavy yawn, looked sleepily about him.

"Tell me that again – once again, just for him to hear," said the Jew, *pointing to Sikes* as he spoke.

"Tell yer what?" *asked the sleepy Noah, shaking himself pettishly.*

"That about – NANCY! You followed her?"

"Yes."

"To London Bridge?"

"Yes."

"Where she met two people?"

"So she did."

"A gentleman and a lady that she had gone to of her own accord before, who asked her to give up all her pals, and Monks first, which *she did* – and to describe him, which *she did* – and to tell her what house it was that we meet at, and go to, which *she did* – and where it could be best watched from, which *she did* – and what time the people went there, which *she did*. *She did all this.* She told it *all*, every word, without a threat, without a murmur – *she did* – did she not?"

"All right," *replied Noah, scratching his head.* "That's just what it was!"

"What did they say about last Sunday?"

"About last Sunday! Why, I told yer that before."

"Again. *Tell it again!*"

"They asked her," as he grew more wakeful, and seemed to have a dawning perception who Sikes was, "they asked her why she didn't come, last Sunday, as she promised. She said she couldn't."

"*Why?* Tell *him* that."

"Because she was forcibly kept at home by Bill – Sikes – the man that she had told them of before."

"What more of him? What more of Bill – Sikes – the man she had told them of before? Tell him that, *tell him that.*"

"Why, that she couldn't very easily get out of doors unless he knew where she was going to, and so the first time she went to see the lady, she – ha! ha! ha! it made me *laugh* when she said it, *that* did – she gave him, a drink *of laudanum*! ha! ha! ha!"

Sikes rushed from the room, and darted up the stairs.

"Bill, *Bill!*" cried Fagin, following him, hastily. "A word. Only a word."

"Let me out. Don't *speak* to me! it's not *safe. Let me out.*"

"Hear me speak a word," rejoined Fagin, *laying his hand upon the lock.* "You won't be – you won't be – *too* – *violent*, Bill?"

The day was breaking, and there was light enough for the men to see each other's faces. They exchanged a brief glance; there was the same fire in the eyes of both.

"I mean, not too – *violent* – for – for – *safety*. Be *crafty*, Bill, and not too *bold*."

The robber dashed into the silent streets.

Without one pause, or moment's consideration; without once turning his head to the right or left; without once raising his eyes to the sky, or lowering them to the ground, but looking straight before him with savage resolution: he muttered not a word, nor relaxed a muscle, until he reached his own house-door. He opened it, *softly*, with a key; strode lightly up the stairs; and entering his own room, *double-locked the door, and drew back the curtain of the bed.*

The girl was lying, half-dressed, upon the bed. He had roused her from her sleep, for she raised herself with a hurried and startled look.

"Get up!"

"It *is* you, Bill!"

"*Get up!!*"

There was a candle burning, but he drew it from the candlestick, and hurled it under the grate. Seeing the faint light of early day without, the girl rose to undraw the curtain.

"*Let it be.* There's light enough for wot I've got to do."

"*Bill, why do you look like that at me?*"

The robber regarded her, for a few seconds, with dilated nostrils and heaving breast; then, grasping her by the head and throat, dragged her into the middle of the room, and placed his heavy hand upon her mouth.

"You were watched tonight, *you she-devil; every word you said was heard.*"

"Then if every word I said was heard, it was heard that I spared you. Bill, *dear Bill*, you cannot have the heart to kill me. Oh! think of all I have given up, only this one night, for *you*. Bill, *Bill*! For dear God's sake, for your own, for mine, stop before you *spill my blood*!! I have been *true* to you, *upon my guilty soul I have*!! The gentleman and that dear lady told me tonight of a home in some foreign country where I could end my days in solitude and peace. Let me see them again, and beg them, on my knees, to show the same mercy to you; and let us both leave this dreadful place, and far apart lead better lives, and forget how we have lived, except in prayers, and never see each other more. It is never too late to repent. They told me so – I feel it now. But we must have *time* – we must have a *little, little time*!"

The house-breaker freed one arm, and grasped his pistol. The certainty of immediate detection if he fired, flashed across his mind; and he beat it twice upon the

upturned face *that almost touched his own.*

She staggered and fell, but raising herself on her knees, *she drew from her bosom a white handkerchief – Rose Maylie's – and holding it up towards Heaven, breathed one prayer, for mercy to her Maker.*

It was a ghastly figure to look upon. The murderer staggering backward to the wall, and shutting out the sight with his hand, seized a heavy club, and *struck her* down!

The bright sun burst upon the crowded city in clear and radiant glory. *Through costly-coloured glass and paper-mended window, through cathedral dome and rotten crevice,* it shed *its equal ray.* It lighted up *the room* where *the murdered woman* lay. It did. He tried to shut it out, but *it would stream in.* If the sight had been a *ghastly* one in the *dull morning,* what was it, *now,* in all that *brilliant light*!!

He had not moved; he had been afraid to stir. There had been a moan and motion of the hand; and, with terror added to rage, he had struck and struck again. Once he threw a rug over it; but it was worse to *fancy* the *eyes,* and imagine them moving towards him, than to see them glaring upward, as if *watching the reflection of the pool of gore that quivered and danced in the sunlight on the ceiling.* He had plucked it off again. And there was the body – mere flesh and blood, no more – but *such* flesh, *and so much blood*!!

He struck a light, kindled a fire, and thrust the club into it. There was hair upon the end, which shrunk into a light cinder, and whirled up the chimney. Even that frightened him; but he held the weapon till it broke, and then piled it on the coals to burn away, and smoulder into ashes. He washed himself, and rubbed his clothes; there were spots upon them that would not be removed, but he cut the pieces out, and burnt them. *How those stains were dispersed about the room! The very feet of his dog were bloody!!*

All this time he had, *never once,* turned his *back* upon the *corpse.* He now moved, *backward,* towards the door: dragging the dog with him, shut the door softly, locked it, took the key, and left the house.

As he gradually left the town behind him all that day, and plunged that night into the solitude and darkness of the country, he was *haunted by that ghastly figure following at his heels.* He could hear its garments rustle in the leaves; and every breath of wind came laden with that last low cry. If *he* stopped, *it* stopped. If *he ran, it followed*; not running too – that would have been a relief – but borne on one slow melancholy air that never rose or fell.

At times, he turned to beat this phantom off, though it should look him dead; but the hair rose on his head, and his blood stood still, for it had turned with him, and was behind him then. He leaned his back against a bank, and felt that it stood above him, visibly out against the cold night sky. He threw himself on his back upon the road. *At his head it*

stood, silent, erect, and still: a human gravestone with its epitaph in Blood!

Suddenly, towards daybreak, he took the desperate resolution of going back to London. "There's somebody to speak to there, at all events. A hiding-place, too, in our gang's old house in Jacob's Island. I'll risk it."

Choosing the least frequented roads for his journey back, he resolved to lie concealed within a short distance of the city until it was dark night again, and then proceed to his destination. He did this, and limped in among three affrighted fellow-thieves, the ghost of himself – blanched face, sunken eyes, hollow cheeks – *his dog at his heels covered with mud, lame, half blind, crawling as if those stains had poisoned him!*

All three men shrank away. Not one of them spake.

"You that keep this house. – Do you mean to sell me, or to let me lie here till the hunt is over?"

"You may stop if you think it safe. But what man ever escaped the men who are after you!"

Hark!! A great sound coming on like a rushing fire! What? *Tracked so soon?* The hunt was up already? Lights gleaming below, voices in loud and earnest talk, hurried tramp of footsteps on the wooden bridges over Folly Ditch, a beating on the heavy door and window-shutters of the house, a waving crowd in the outer darkness like a field of corn moved by an angry storm!

"The tide was in, as I come up. Give me a rope. I may drop from the top of the house, at the back into the Folly Ditch, and clear off that way, or be stifled. *Give me a rope!*"

No one stirred. They pointed to where they kept such things, and the murderer hurried with a strong cord to the housetop. *Of all the terrific yells* that ever fell on *mortal ears, none could exceed* the furious cry when *he was seen.* Some shouted to those who were nearest, to set the house on fire; others adjured the officers to shoot him dead; others, with execrations, clutched and tore at him in the empty air; some called for ladders, some for sledge-hammers; some ran with torches to and fro, to seek them. "*I promise Fifty Pounds,*" cried Mr. Brownlow from the nearest bridge, "*to the man who takes that murderer alive!*"

He set his foot against the stack of chimneys, fastened one end of the rope firmly round it, and with the other made a strong running noose by the aid of his hands and teeth. With the cord round his back, he could let himself down to within a less distance of the ground than his own height, and had his knife ready in his hand to cut the cord, and drop.

At the instant that he brought the loop over his head before slipping it beneath his arm-pits, *looking behind him* on the *roof* he *threw up his arms, and yelled, "The eyes again!"* Staggering as if struck by lightning, he lost his balance and tumbled over the parapet. The noose was at his neck; it ran up with his weight; tight as a bowstring, and swift as the arrow it speeds.

He fell five-and-thirty feet, and hung with his open *knife clenched in his stiffening hand*!!

The *dog* which had lain concealed till now, ran backwards and forwards on the parapet with a dismal howl, and, collecting himself for a spring, jumped for the *dead man's shoulders*. Missing his aim, he fell into the ditch, turning over as he went, and striking against a stone, *dashed out his brains*!

"CAPTAIN CHARLES JOHNSON" (DANIEL DEFOE 1660–1731)

Three Infamous Pirates

(from *A General History Of The Robberies and Murders of the Most Notorious Pyrates*, 1724)

The real author of this book was only discovered about fifty years ago when Defoe's handwriting was recognised. He is famous to us as the author of **Robinson Crusoe** *and* **Moll Flanders** *and was a prolific writer and journalist. Piracy has often had a glamorous edge to it: but the grand adventures of Drake and Hawkins in the sixteenth century had degenerated into atrocities, though the captains were still celebrated as larger than life characters. The extract on Captain Teach (Blackbeard) is typical of this. The other extracts, celebrating two female pirates, are sensational in a different way.*

Captain Teach alias Blackbeard

CAPTAIN TEACH, assumed the Cognomen of *Blackbeard*, from that large Quantity of Hair, which, like a frightful Meteor, covered his whole Face, and frightened *America* more than any Comet that has appeared there a long Time.

This Beard was black, which he suffered to grow of an extravagant Length; as to Breadth, it came up to his Eyes; he was accustomed to twist it with Ribbons, in small Tails, after the Manner of our Ramilies Wiggs, and turn them about his Ears: in Time of Action, he wore a Sling over his Shoulders, with three Brace of Pistols, hanging in Holsters like Bandaliers; and stuck lighted Matches under his Hat, which appearing on each Side of his Face, his Eyes naturally looking fierce and wild, made him altogether such a Figure, that Imagination cannot form an Idea of a Fury, from Hell, to look more frightful.

Blackbeard the Pyrate

Mary Read

IN THEIR Cruise they [Mary Read's crew] took a great Number of Ships belonging to Jamaica, and other Parts of the West Indies, bound to and from England; and whenever they met any good Artist, or other Person that might be of any great Use to their Company, if he was not willing to enter, it was their Custom to keep him by Force. Among these was a young Fellow of a most engaging Behaviour, or, at least, he was so in the Eyes of Mary Read, who became so smitten with his Person and Address, that she could neither rest Night or Day. . .

It happened this young Fellow had a Quarrel with one of the Pyrates, and their Ship then lying at an Anchor, near one of the Islands, they had appointed to go ashore and fight, according to the Custom of the Pyrates: Mary Read was to the last Degree uneasy and anxious, for the Fate of her Lover; she would not have had him refuse the Challenge, because, she could not bear the Thoughts of his being branded with Cowardice; on the other Side, she dreaded the Event, and apprehended the Fellow might be too hard for him: . . . she took a Resolution of quarrelling with this Fellow herself, and having challenged him ashore, she appointed the Time two Hours sooner than that when he was to meet her Lover, where she fought him at Sword and Pistol, and killed him upon the Spot.

It is true, she had fought before, when she had been insulted by some of those Fellows, but now it was altogether in her Lover's Cause, she stood as it were betwixt him and Death, as if she could not live without him. If he had no regard for her before, this Action would have bound him to her for ever; but there was no Occasion for Ties or Obligation, his Inclination towards her was sufficient; in fine, they plighted their Troth to each other, which Mary Read said, she look'd upon to be as good a Marriage, in Conscience, as if it had been done by a Minister in Church; and to this was owing her great Belly, which she pleaded to save her Life.

It is no doubt, but many had Compassion for her, yet the Court could not avoid finding her Guilty; for among other Things, one of the Evidences against her, deposed, that being taken by Rackam, and detain'd some Time on board, he fell accidentally into Discourse with Mary Read, whom he taking for a young Man, ask'd her, what Pleasure she could have in being concerned in such Enterprises, where her Life was continually in Danger, by Fire or Sword; and not only so, but she must be sure of dying an ignominious Death, if she should be taken alive? – She answer'd, that as to hanging, she thought it no great Hardship, for, were it not for that, every cowardly Fellow would turn Pyrate, and so infest the Seas, that Men of Courage must starve: that if it was

The two infamous female pirates, Mary Read and Anne Bonny

put to the Choice of the Pyrates, they would not have the Punishment
less than Death, the Fear of which kept some dastardly Rogues honest;
that many of those who are now cheating the Widows and Orphans, and
oppressing their poor Neighbours, who have no Money to obtain Justice,
would then rob at Sea, and the Ocean would be crowded with Rogues,
like the Land, and no Merchant would venture out; so that the Trade, in
a little Time, would not be worth following.

Anne Bonny

S HE BECAME acquainted with Rackam the Pyrate, who making Court-ship to her, soon found Means of withdrawing her Affections from her Husband, so that she consented to elope from him, and go to Sea with Rackam in Men's Cloaths: she was as good as her Word, and after she had been at Sea some Time, she proved with Child, and beginning to grow big, Rackam landed her on the Island of Cuba; and recommending her there to some Friends of his, they took Care of her, till she was brought to Bed: When she was up and well again, he sent for her to bear him Company.

The King's Proclamation being out, for pardoning of Pyrates, he took the Benefit of it, and surrender'd; afterwards being sent upon the privateering Account, he return'd to his old Trade . . . In all these Expeditions, Anne Bonny bore him Company, and when any Business was to be done in their Way, no Body was more forward or courageous than she, and particularly when they were taken; she and Mary Read, with one more, were all the Persons that durst keep the Deck, as has been before hinted . . . The Day that Rackam was executed, by special Favour, he was admitted to see her; but all the Comfort she gave him, was, *that she was sorry to see him there, but if he had fought like a Man, he need not have been hang'd like a Dog.*

She was continued in Prison, to the Time of her lying in, and afterwards reprieved from Time to Time; but what is become of her since, we cannot tell; only this we know, that she was not executed.

SIR WALTER RALEIGH (1552–1618)

Even Such is Time (1618)

Raleigh was a courtier, soldier, sailor and writer. He named the colony of Virginia, sailed to look for El Dorado, fought the Spanish and introduced the cultivation of the potato. He came close to execution at other times before finally losing favour. He wrote this poem on the eve of his execution. To write so simply and directly after such a life, at such a time, seems remarkable.

EVEN SUCH is Time, which takes in trust
  Our youth, and joys, and all we have;
And pays us but with age and dust,
    Which, in the dark and silent grave,

When we have wandered all our ways,
  Shuts up the story of our days:
    And from which earth, and grave, and dust,
    The Lord shall raise me up, I trust.

Sir Walter Raleigh's execution

JOSEPH LANCASTER (1778–1838)

Improvements in Education (1806)

At a time when the education of the poor was almost entirely neglected, Joseph Lancaster began to teach them for free. When the numbers became too great he set up a school and the monitorial system where older pupils acted as young teachers drilling the children in highly mechanical ways. The schools were popular and this extract does him little justice although, on its own, the description of these outrageous and ingenious punishments is wonderfully out of key with our own views and practices – at the moment.

THAT CHILDREN should idle away their time, or talk in school, is very improper – they cannot talk and learn at the same time. In my school talking is considered as an offence; and yet it occurs very seldom, in proportion to the number of children: whenever this happens to be the case, an appropriate punishment succeeds.

Each monitor of a class is responsible for the cleanliness, order, and quietness of those under him. He is also a lad of unimpeachable veracity – a qualification on which much depends. He should have a continual eye over every one in the class under his care, and notice when a boy is loitering away his time in talking or idleness. Having thus seen, he is bound in duty to lodge an accusation against him for *misdemeanor*. In order to do this silently, he has a number of cards, written on differently: as, "I have seen this boy idle," – "I have seen this boy talking," etc. This rule applies to every class, and each card has the name of the particular class written thereon: so that, by seeing a card written on as above, belonging to the first or sixth, or any other reading class, it is immediately known who is the monitor that is the accuser. This card is given to the defaulter, and he is required to present it at the head of the school – a regulation that must be complied with. On a repeated or frequent offence, after admonition has failed, the lad to whom he presents the card has liberty to put a wooden log round his neck, which serves him as a pillory, and with this he is sent to his seat. This machine may weight from four to six pounds, some more and some less. The neck is not pinched or closely confined – it is chiefly burthensome by the manner in which it encumbers the neck, when the delinquent turns to the right or left. While it rests on his shoulders, the equilibrium is preserved; but, on the least motion one way or the other, it is lost, and the logs operate as a dead weight upon the neck. Thus, he is confined to sit in his proper position. If this is unavailing, it is common to fasten the legs of offenders together with wooden shackles: one or more, according to the offence. The *shackle* is a piece of wood about a foot, sometimes six or eight inches long, and tied to each leg. When shackled, he cannot walk but in a very slow, measured pace: being obliged to take six steps, when confined, for two when at liberty. Thus accoutred, he is ordered to walk round the school-room, till tired out – he is glad to sue for liberty, and promise *his endeavour* to behave more steadily in future. Should not this punishment have the desired effect, the left hand is tied behind the back, or wooden shackles fastened from elbow to elbow, behind the back. Sometimes the legs are tied together. Occasionally boys are put in a sack, or in a basket, suspended to the roof of the school, in the sight of all the pupils, who frequently smile at *the birds in the cage*. This punishment is one of the most terrible that can be inflicted on boys of sense and abilities. Above all, it is dreaded by the monitors: the name of it is sufficient, and therefore it is but seldom resorted to on their account. Frequent or old offenders are yoked together sometimes, by a piece of wood that fastens round all their necks: and, thus confined, they parade the school, walking backwards – being obliged to pay very great attention to their footsteps, for fear of running against any object that might cause the yoke to hurt their necks, or to keep from falling down. Four or six can be yoked together this way.

When a boy is disobedient to his parents, profane in his language, or has committed any offence against morality, or is remarkable for slovenliness, it is usual for him to be dressed up with labels, describing his offence, and a tin or paper crown on his head. In that manner he walks round the school, two boys preceding him, and proclaiming his fault; varying the proclamation according to the different offences. When a boy comes to school with dirty face or hands, and it seems to be more the effect of habit than of accident, a girl is appointed to wash his face in the sight of the whole school. This usually creates much diversion, especially when (as previously directed) she gives his cheeks a few *gentle strokes of correction* with her hand. The same event takes place as to girls, when in habits of slothfulness. Occasionally, such offenders against cleanliness walk round the school, preceded by a boy proclaiming her fault – and the same as to the boys. A proceeding that usually turns the *public spirit* of the whole school against the culprit.

Few punishments are so effectual as confinement after school hours. It is, however, attended with one unpleasant circumstance. In order to confine the bad boys in the school-room, after school-hours, it is often needful the master, or some proper substitute for him, should confine himself in school, to keep them in order. This inconvenience may be avoided, by tying them to the desks, in such a manner that they cannot untie themselves. These variations in the *modes* of *unavoidable punishment* give it the continual force of novelty, whatever shape it may assume. Any single kind of punishment, continued constantly in use, becomes familiar, and loses its effect. Nothing but variety can continue the power of novelty.

JONATHAN WILD (c. 1683–1725)

The Thief-Taker General

Living up to his name, Wild established himself as one of the most famous of criminals, hitting on the ingenious device of collecting rewards as a very effective thief-catcher — mostly people who had defied him in some way or hadn't stolen enough. He is celebrated as the central character of a novel by Henry Fielding. Defoe wrote a book about him and he features in "The Beggar's Opera". Eventually his crimes became too outrageous and his luck ran out.

The crimes of Jonathan Wild

1. It appears by several Informations upon Oath, that Jonathan Wild hath, for many Years past, been a Confederate with great Numbers of Highwaymen, Pick-pockets, House-breakers, Shop-lifters, and other Thieves.

2. That he hath form'd a kind of Corporation of Thieves, of which he is the Head or Director, and that notwithstanding his pretended Services in detecting and prosecuting Offenders, he procured such only to be hang'd as conceal'd their Booty or refused to share it with him.

3. That he hath divided the Town and Country into so many Districts, and appointed distinct Gangs for each, who regularly accounted with him for their Robberies. He had also a particular Set to steal at Churches in Time of divine Service, and also other moving Detachments to attend at Court on Birth-Days, Balls, etc. and upon both Houses of Parliament, Circuits, and Country Fairs.

4. That the Persons employ'd by him were for the most part Felons Convict, who have return'd from Transportation before the Time for which they were transported was expired, and that he made Choice of them to be his Agents, because they could not be legal Evidence against him, and because he had it in his Power to take from them what Part of the stolen Goods he thought fit, and otherwise use them ill, or hang them, as he pleased.

5. That he hath from Time to Time supplied such convicted Felons with Money and Cloaths, and lodged them in his own House, the better

A mock "ticket" for Wild's execution

to conceal them, particularly some against whom there are now Informations for diminishing and counterfeiting Broad-Pieces and Guineas.

6. That he hath not only been a Receiver of stolen Goods, as well as of Writings of all Kinds for near fifteen Years last past, but frequently been a Confederate, and robb'd along with the above-mentioned convicted Felons.

7. That in order to carry on these vile Practises to gain some Credit with the ignorant Multitude, he usually carried about him a short Silver Staff, as a Badge of Authority from the Government, which he used to produce when he himself was concerned in robbing.

8. That he had under his Care and Direction several Warehouses for receiving and concealing stolen Goods; and also a Ship for carrying off Jewels, Watches, and other valuable Goods to Holland, where he hath a superannuated Thief for his Factor.

9. That he kept in Pay several Artists to make Alterations, and transform Watches, Seals, Snuff-Boxes, Rings, and other valuable Things, that they might not be known, several of which he used to present to such Persons as he thought might be of Service to him.

10. That he seldom or ever helped the Owners to their Notes and Papers they had lost, unless he found them able exactly to specify and describe them, and then often insisted on more than half the Value.

11. Lastly, it appears that he hath frequently sold human Blood, by procuring false Evidence to swear Persons into Facts they were not guilty of, sometimes to prevent them from being Evidence against himself; at others, for the sake of the great Reward given by the Government.

The Humble Petition of Jonathan Wild

Humbly Presented to His Majesty, on

Wednesday May the 19th at

His Royal Palace at St. James's

May it please Your Majesty:

'Tis nothing but your Majesty's wonted Goodness and Clemency that could encourage me to sue for your Royal Favour and Pardon, and make me presume so far on the same as to dare to offer this my most Humble Petition to Your Majesty's serene Consideration. For Since Your Majesty has many Times been graciously pleased to spare the Lives of even Traitors themselves I cannot but hope for a Reprieve from so good a Prince whom I can esteem no less than an inexhaustible Fountain of Mercy; wherefore, most Dread and August Sovereign, humbly prostrating myself at your Royal Feet I presume to set forth my wicked and melancholy Circumstances and from your Bounty to seek that Favour which is nowhere else to be found.

I have indeed been a most wicked and notorious Offender, but was never Guilty of or inclin'd to Treasonable Practices or Murder, both of which I ever had in the utmost Detestation and Abhorrence which affords me great Comfort in the midst of my Calamity and Affliction.

I have a sickly Wife loaded with Grief who must inevitably come to the Grave with me if I suffer; or lead a most miserable Life, she being already *non compos Mentis*.

If I receive Your Majesty's Royal Favour of a Reprieve I do firmly resolve to relinquish my wicked Ways and to detest (as far as in me lays) all such who shall persevere therein, as a Testimony of which I have a List ready to show to such whom your Majesty shall appoint to see it, which is all that can be offered by Your Majesty's most dutiful, Loyal, and Obedient Petitioner,

Newgate, May the 19th 1725.

J. WILD

ROBERT SOUTHEY (1774–1843)

Bishop Hatto

Southey based his poem on medieval tales which record that the Bishop of Mainz (968–970) burnt people alive in a barn after catching them stealing corn in a famine. He compared their dying screams to the squeaking of mice and, legend has it, built the Mäuseturm (the Mouse Tower) on a rock in the Rhine to escape revenge.

THE SUMMER and autumn had been so wet,
That in winter the corn was growing yet,
'Twas a piteous sight to see all around
The corn lie rotting on the ground.

Every day the starving poor
They crowded around Bishop Hatto's door,
For he had a plentiful last year's store,
And all the neighbourhood could tell
His granaries were furnished well.

At last Bishop Hatto appointed a day
To quiet the poor without delay,
He bade them to his great barn repair,
And they should have food for the winter there.

Rejoiced the tidings good to hear,
The poor folks flock'd from far and near,
The great barn was full as it could hold
Of women and children, and young and old.

Then when he saw it could hold no more,
Bishop Hatto he made fast the door,
And whilst for mercy on Christ they call,
He set fire to the barn and burnt them all.

"I' faith, 'tis an excellent bonfire!" quoth he,
"And the country is greatly obliged to me,
For ridding it in these times forlorn
Of rats that only consume the corn."

So then to his palace returnèd he,
And he sate down to supper merrily,
And he slept that night like an innocent man;
But Bishop Hatto never slept again.

In the morning as he enter'd the hall,
Where his picture hung against the wall,
A sweat like death all over him came,
For the rats had eaten it out of the frame.

As he look'd there came a man from his farm,
He had a countenance white with alarm.
"My lord, I open'd your granaries this morn,
And the rats had eaten all your corn."

Another came running presently,
And he was pale as pale could be,
"Fly! my Lord Bishop, fly!" quoth he,
"Ten thousand rats are coming this way –
The Lord forgive you for yesterday!"

"I'll go to my tower on the Rhine," replied he,
"'Tis the safest place in Germany;
The walls are high, and the shores are steep,
And the tide is strong, and the water deep."

Bishop Hatto fearfully hasten'd away,
And he cross'd the Rhine without delay,
And reach'd his tower in the island, and barr'd
All the gates secure and hard.

He laid him down and closed his eyes –
But soon a scream made him arise.
He started, and saw two eyes of flame
On his pillow, from whence the screaming came.

He listen'd and look'd; – it was only the cat;
But the Bishop he grew more fearful for that,
For she sat screaming, mad with fear,
At the army of rats that were drawing near.

For they have swum over the river so deep,
And they have climb'd the shores so steep,
And now by thousands up they crawl
To the holes and windows in the wall.

Down on his knees the bishop fell,
And faster and faster his beads did he tell,
As louder and louder drawing near
The saw of their teeth without he could hear.

And in at the windows, and in at the door,
And through the walls, by thousands they pour,
And down from the ceiling, and up through the floor,
From the right and the left, from behind and before,
From within and without, from above and below,
And all at once to the Bishop they go.

They have whetted their teeth against the stones,
And now they pick the Bishop's bones;
They gnawed the flesh from every limb,
For they were sent to do judgement on him!

ANON

The Wicked who would do me Harm
(translated from the Gaelic by
A. Carmichael)

*Sticks and stones may break my bones but words . . . This is a marvellous army
of words doing battle and giving due warning to anyone who threatens. It's
wonderful to read, to turn the words and phrases over and sound them out
aloud. And what a relief for anger . . .*

THE WICKED who would do me harm
  May he take the throat disease,
Globularly, spirally, circularly,
Fluxy, pellety, horny-grim.

Be it harder than the stone,
Be it blacker than the coal,
Be it swifter than the duck,
Be it heavier than the lead.

Be it fiercer, fiercer, sharper, harsher, more malignant,
Than the hard, wound-quivering holly,
Be it sourer than the sained, lustrous, bitter, salt salt,
Seven seven times.

Oscillating thither,
Undulating hither,
Staggering downwards,
Floundering upwards.

Drivelling outwards,
Snivelling inwards,
Oft hurrying out,
Seldom coming in.

A wisp the portion of each hand,
A foot in the base of each pillar,
A leg the prop of each jamb,
A flux driving and dragging him.

A dysentery of blood from heart, from form, from bones,
From the liver, from the lobe, from the lungs,
And a searching of veins, of throat, and of kidneys,
To my contemners and traducers.

In name of the God of might,
Who warded from me every evil,
And who shielded me in strength,
From the net of my breakers
    And destroyers.